A SOUNDLESS DAWN

DUSTIN LaVALLEY

SINISTER GRIN PRESS

MMXVII

AUSTIN, TEXAS

Sinister Grin Press

Austin, TX

www.sinistergrinpress.com

March 2017

Cover Art by Matt Davis

Book Design by Travis Tarpley

ISBN: 978-1-944044-39-8

For my father, who kept us safe.

ACKNOWLEDGEMENTS

Special thanks to Lee, Dallas, Jerry, and Tom

Contents

INTRODUCTION TO *A SOUNDLESS DAWN* BY EDWARD LEE

Don't get me wrong; I have nothing to sound derogatory or cynical about with regard to modern horror fiction. It's easily criticized for its formulaic nomenclature, much the same as horror films are criticized. "There's nothing original anymore! Writers have no creativity of their own! Every story mimics other stories; everything's a sequel, everything's a remake, everything's vampires, everything's friggin' zombies, everything's a haunted house full of camcorders! Dag nabbit, when are writers going to stop writing what's already been written and come up with ideas that have never before been encountered by readers/viewers?"

The answer to this question is "never," and the reason is quite legitimate, and here is what many critics either don't understand or willingly ignore (otherwise they'd have little to write about!) Formula equals Familiarity, and Familiarity equals Trust. When I pick a book to read, I need to trust that there's a high order of likelihood that I'll enjoy it. For example, I love haunted house stories. I read them ALL THE TIME, and any DVD that pops up with a haunted-looking house on it–yes sir!– I plunk down my money. Haunted house stories go back a long way, but let's just say that the first "formula" haunted house piece was Edward Bulwer-Lytton's, "The House and the Brain," written in 1855 or thereabouts. Specifically, it's about people investigating a house reputed to be haunted. Sound familiar? You bet it does, and since that time there have been COUNTLESS other stories about people investigating houses reputed to be haunted. The reason is simple.

Readers LIKE stories about people investigating houses reputed to be haunted! The FAMILIARITY of the FORMULA gives the lover of such tales enough of a sense of TRUST to buy the book, story, movie, comic, or what have you. Contrary to a good many critics who dismiss commercial or "genre" fiction as bunk, a FORMULA is a crucial ingredient to serviceable entertainment. Let's be abstract a moment: if writing formula stories was a crime, then I'd be on Death Row. So would everyone from Stephen King to William Shakespeare. From the—oh, I'll go ahead and use the word—aesthetic point of view, formula is the marketing flag. From an allegorical point of view, formula is the "foundation" and plot is the "house." You lay a solid, trustworthy foundation, and on it you build an exciting, new kind of house. Didn't Stephen King once call it pouring new wine into old bottles? The old bottle is the formula, the new wine is the plot/setting/exposition/characters/etc., that tastes different, and hopefully better, than the wine of the past. Hence, when critics cynically say "Do we REALLY need another zombie novel?" or "Do we REALLY need another vampire movie?" the answer is "yes," for as long as authors do interesting, new, and relatable things with those formulae, and for as long as their creativity propels them to pursue variations and angles and events that put fresh, delicious "icing" on those old, beloved "cakes."

Which brings me to Dustin LaValley and his collection, A SOUNDLESS DAWN. I've encumbered you with the above 480ish words of my personal philosophy about genre fiction not to make a point but instead to make a counter-point. In my aforementioned legitimization of the formulaic, there's one aspect of the business I forgot to retail to you: it's a lot easier to write than the fiction we call "speculative," or "literary," or "artistic," or "avant-garde," or "existentially relevant," and so on. THAT'S the kind of fiction that most defines what we are via any number of demonstrations of theme, such as (I'll semi-quote one of my English professors from 30-odd years ago) humankind's purpose in our age, humankind's discovery of self-actualization in an un-actualized social realm, the spiritual versus the naturalistic, the reckoning of the conscience (or the rejection of it), the ascension of individual identity above the masses (or the disavowal of it), and—wow, there were a lot of such demonstrations but I can't remember them all now. (Incidentally, he DIDN'T say man's inhumanity to man, thank God!) That professor was a pretty sharp guy; I think his name was Thomas Webner. Anyway, my point-within-a-point is thus: fiction that makes provocative observations such as those on the good professor's list, is fiction that is far more important and thought-worthy than zombies, vampires, monsters, people investigating houses reputed to be haunted, and the rest of what we call escape fare. We read escape fiction for just that, the desire to ESCAPE from the doldrums, stresses, disappointments, and outrages of the REAL world and spend some entertaining time in an UNreal world. We read non-genre fiction (because there is no definitive name for it, I don't think) to remind us about the real things in life and the aspects of that reality which shape us into the complex, diversified, (and also the tragically flawed), organisms that we exist and walk the earth as; not to ESCAPE from but instead to come to grips with all those doldrums, stresses, disappointments, etc. I'm talking about fiction that makes cogent points which fuel our sense of introspection, invites self-examination and resultant deduction, triggers our awareness of causes and effects--fiction that is "important." In order to help us understand these elements and the reasons why we NEED to understand them, the good professor had us read the works of, to name a few, James Joyce, William Faulkner, Jean-Paul Sartre, Henrik Ibsen, and Franz Kafka. Few will argue that writers such as these represent the cream of the literary crop because their work doesn't necessarily entertain us at all but instead teaches us something about real life and what being human is all about.

The stories in A SOUNDLESS DAWN teach us something about real life and what being human is all about. If the tales in this book should be called horror fiction, it is foremost NOT the kind of horror we associate with this term. Not the horror of bumps in the night, nor of trans-vagina eviscerations, nor of monsters with a serious case of the ass, but the horror of the modern psyche, the elan, the "vitale of life," or whatever that thing really is which inseparably identifies us as life forms exclusive from all others. When I read this book, the no-pussyfooting prose and the power of its messages forced me at once to think of writers like Hubert Selby, Harry Crews, Raymond Carver, the venerable William Burroughs; it forced me to think of taglines like "contaminated realism," "minimalism-as-psychical-glut," "auto-parasitism," "cracked-mirror rite of passage," "cataclysmic domesticity," and the like. This is not pulp fare, folks–this is compelling literature, and in these works with the epiphanies they invite, you'll find observations that dare to step past much of what we've seen lately in the circles of all things aesthetic. Here is a portrayal of the undertows of the animus seldom demonstrated in literature of the distant and recent past. To call this book stunning, marvelous, and original is plainly accurate but it's also quite facile, because those adjectives don't come close to conveying its uniqueness and, yes, its importance. I don't know that I've ever read a collection as wholly its own as this, nor a collection so absolutely unconnected to what's been done before; in fact, it's been a long, long time since I've had the privilege to immerse myself into a book more full of the human soul than this.

If you want gut-slinging, blood-gulping, mansions full of naked ghosts and libidinous monsters, reach for Edward Lee. If you want the written word as an art form, reach for A SOUNDLESS DAWN by Dustin LaValley.

–Edward Lee, author of *Haunted House*

THE CITY THAT BLEEDS

This city's streetlights bleed. Golden memories drip and fade on worn, weathered concrete. Fluorescence left to bubble in the summer heat, sticking to the souls of corner-girls and John Does.

A Full Chamber and a Smile

Humanity has become a very sad perversion, save those of us who stand outside the norm and demand change and strive for individuality, creativity in the arts and above all, education equality for the masses. This Taco Bell generation is playing Russian Roulette with a full chamber and a smile.

Buffalo, NY

When I was a child my parents packed the kids into their brown station wagon and drove west, towards the cold winds off of a giant lake I did not know the name of. To this very day, I do not remember what the reason was for us children to suffer in that cold grey of winter, but I sure as shit remember the hell that was Buffalo.

PICTURE-IN-PICTURE

He runs...

A boy of ten-years-old, wearing a faded flannel shirt, dirty blue jeans, sneakers and a wool cap on his head of short dark hair runs along the sidewalk of a street ignored by time. The houses stuck in the golden age between the birth of baby-boomers and the Korean War. The paint on their full porches chipped and the wood splintered. No distinction between the next and the last other than the pattern of decay. Ripping through the air like lightning, feet stomping the ground like thunder, he huffs and puffs and his chest rises and falls with each breath. His adolescent energy pushed to its margin by fear, confusion and horror.

The boy continues to run as he and his world are brought up to the corner in a small box to allow a dirty man in a clean room to appear in full-screen. In that corner the boy runs, never stopping or slowing. He runs and he runs and he runs...

The dirty man, his best clothes on his back soiled and tattered sits slouched in a wooden chair, its legs creak as he adjusts his weight. The room, whitewashed, bland and sterile is empty and devoid of any and all things living besides this man and his story. A juxtaposition of extremes: the man and the room, the cleanliness of the air and the filthiness of his voice. Side by side they couldn't have less connection...

"Blood is the fuel of life. Women are said to be at their wildest during their menstruation. I've never had a problem with a little blood. Period sex has its ups and downs. Well, no I guess if you don't mind blood it's all positive. I don't mind. Blood that is, never bothered me. Some people are bothered by only their own blood, others the other way 'round. But me, nah, neither one. I could bleed or make another bleed, blood is blood to me. Sex though... I've had my share. Oh, have I had my share. I've seen some messed up fetishes and I don't mind, really. You want a donkey, a steamer, another man, another woman, a lady-boy... I don't mind, never been one to pass judgment. Rough, loud, hair-tugging tit-smacking bound and gagged, blind-folded, hands on neck good old assertive, dominative sex. Now that's what fucking is about! A little blood comes by the hand... that's just a sign of good sex. A lot of people don't even know what sex is, they lie on top of each other, that's what they do. That's not sex. It's blood, sweat, bitten collarbones and swollen ass cheeks. That's sex. It's like a drug, good sex that is. And drugs, they only make it even better. Not a damn thing wrong with sex and drugs. Not a damn thing wrong with drugs at that...

The box in the corner fades to black and from within that darkness, a picture comes in clear...

In a quickened pace the young boy weaves through his home, past darkened rooms without doors and doorways standing with a slant... broken and buckled foundation beams giving the stained, discolored walls a feel of unease to any unsuspecting visitor. His feet come to a stop and he fumbles with the doorknob of a bedroom. It opens and he takes a step inside, a room lit neon orange by a sign of a beer logo. He hesitates, ready to go forth but stalling at the sight of his parents. Beautiful is his mother, ugly his father-

figure ··the house's self-proclaimed ruler·· in the nude. She rides him, bare skin glossy in the light. Large, soft breasts sway across a trim stomach as she gyrates against his thrusts. Her long, curly blonde hair tickles the arch of her back as she lets her head loll side to side.

For the boy, the moment between first sight and reaction of the man who claims to be ruler and father plays out like hours. He grabs an empty bottle, yells and tosses it at the child. Though caught aghast, the boy ducks in time for the glass to crash against the hallway wall. He witnesses his mother's face contort into a horrid display of befuddled anger and he shuts the door as she yells, 'Get the fuck out!'

The boy retreats, searching for an exit he seems lost in his own home. Slowing for doorways that he does not enter, eyeing the darkness for a way out before continuing on.

He runs and as he runs...

The dirty man in the chair continues his story on the large main screen.

...LSD, Lysergic Acid Diethylamide, acid. Ain't nothing can top that. Let me trip, leave me there, I'll be fine. Weed, nah, not my top choice but nothing wrong with a bubbling bong, nothing wrong with hash cakes. Too tame, never did a thing for me. Pity what the hippies did to that wonder drug. Dirty, filthy fucking hippies! It's non-addictive and beneficial for pain, used by all sorts for all sorts of ailments from cancer to headaches, anxiety to depression. Man, those filthy fucking hippies ruined it for everyone. Okay not all of us, but those of us too scared to find it these days. Of course, there are side effects but nothing compared to the shit kids are injecting and now those synthetic bath salts. Jesus, compared to other drugs today, weed is candy cigarettes...

The picture in the corner, the small box containing the child once again shows him on the sidewalk of his neighborhood. His sneakers meet the crumbling, uneven concrete with urgency as he runs and runs...

...Sticking needles in your arm, now that's fucked. Never been any good reasons so stick a needle in your arm. There's too much risk in that, too much risk. People these days, they're disgusting. The rich, the poor, doesn't matter who, they're filled with all sorts of shit. Aids, HIV, Hep-B, the list goes on and on. List so long it's impossible to know of 'em all. Leave the needles alone or you'll end up with some whore's needle sticking in your arm injecting AIDS into yourself. Boom! Death-warrant signed...

The picture of the boy repeats, it sizzles and pops in a snowfall. Frames climb the screen. The same few milliseconds of images replay like celluloid unraveling from the spool or a bad connection on a local television station during an electrical storm. Then, it clicks, and the boy is walking up the stairs of a house similar to his own, similar to all the homes on the street which are similar to all the homes in the neighborhood. The door is ajar; noise spills out of the space and he opens it just enough to sidestep inside.

Music envelopes the boy as do billows of smoke. The house is illuminated with red, green, blue and other various colored lighting. His rush comes to a halt. He stands in the middle of a room surrounded by teenagers and twenty-somethings partying. An orgy of drugs hard and soft and alcohol fruity and straight, men and women between the wisps and behind the strobes, many are melted into one another --hands roaming and tongues prodding-- in make-out sessions and future regrets. The fear, the confusion and helplessness remains on his face as he scans the foreign land for a familiar body.

There is technical trouble again as the picture freezes on the boy's expression and the man in the whiteness speaks of demise.

...Death. Now that's something you can't touch on without some self-righteous, religious pecker-head telling you you're wrong no matter what you believe in. Atheist, Christian, Muslim, Jewish, Agnostic, we all die. There's no pearly gates, no hundred virgins, no kingdom in the heavens, no Santa Claus or Easter Bunny. You die and you're dead, nothing more. Worm food, one with the soil, ash off the cliff...

The box in the corner begins to skip. Forward, backward, possibly sideways it is not known.

The boy sits on the back porch. His hands stuffed in his pockets, his legs dangling and eyes on the ground. He is caught in thought when he flinches and whips his head up and towards the sound of a pop. A few beats pass before he drops down to the ground and begins to walk in the direction from where the noise came. His head down, watching his sneakers scuff the ground as he walks, hands deep in those pockets he takes his time.

As the boy approaches to the garage in what seems to be the same lapping image, the dirty man's story in the talking picture interrupts.

...It's like going to sleep I imagine. Sleeping without dreaming. You ever have a night with no dreams? Then you know what death feels like. The process of dying, that's something else. Dying can be long and drawn out, painful or quick and over with. Not always your choice but if you had the choice, if I had the choice? Shit, I don't know. I figure if I was going slowly in pain, I'd drug myself up like they do those terminal cancer patients. Load 'em up so high they don't give two shits...

The boy in the corner reaches the garage. It takes his whole strength to open one of the large, double-wide doors. They're outdated, more fitting for that of a barn as it once was. Now used as a two car hold and workstation. The light of the fading sun casts a cockeyed shadow across a body slumped against the tool bench and the paved floor. The boy wanders forth and stares at his older brother. Blood pours from his mouth, ears and nose. At the end of an extended arm, a .38 revolver is stuck in his right hand. The index finger curled in the trigger guard. The boy mutters a name and of course, there is no response. He makes a small step and as he does so, gently nudges his brother's sprawled out legs. The dead boy's upper body slides down, following the momentum of his head which meets the floor with a wet thump.

The boy turns and is about to burst into a frantic run when the box freezes. The moving picture paused by an unseen force with access to remote viewing. He is not much unlike a two-dimensional stick-figure giving chase or being pursued.

The man, again... the dirty man in the sterile room stays on topic.

...Sometimes I think about death. Not about dying or what happens after or before, but death itself. You know, like what color is death? What's its story? Is death religious, does it believe in a god or gods or is it a secular humanist? Does it like music, if so what kind? You'd think metal, something heavy and fast, right? Something that might cause you to go out blazing, suicide by cop or depress you enough to overdose on sleeping pills. Is it political? Does death have a seat in the GOP, does it ride a pink elephant? This is the stuff the mind wonders but no one talks about. Masturbation is a thing of the past, we're all open to it now, it's not hush-hush anymore but this, what death is, this no one talks about. Why not? Fear. We fear and we keep our mouths shut. Otherwise we might end up some bumbling, stinky crackpot on the street. Shunned by society and burdened by cultural norms. Beggars and bums...

Pause is removed and in a flash the boy is gone, sprinting from the garage and down the driveway. He is up the back stairs and through the back door as if... as if he has just seen a dead man...

...Sweat-pan money. That's what life is about for some. Bums and beggars, roaches and rats is what we are. We're not people, we're not human beings, we're vermin and we're trash. We're on the street and the street is hard. Street life, ain't nothing harder than a street life. Gotta be shameless, can't have dignity. If you do, it's taken from you, stripped, skin becomes hard as steel. It's gotta be. If you have too much pride to ask a passerby for a few bucks, some change, a cigarette, you're done. You can't have pride, it's gone. You're shameless, you're stripped nude and naked...

As if taken from a parallel dimension or a deleted scene, up in the corner box, the slightly altered progression

*to his parent's room for the boy is in a more ardent manner.
The paint has flow and matches the trim, the house stands
without a slant and when he opens the door to the bedroom
they are moaning in the dark. No neon lighting, no nude
bodies only darkness and the sounds of lovemaking. He
shuts the door, fast, but unnoticed by the two inside. There
is no beer bottle flung and no yelling to chase him as he
runs through the house the way from which he came.
Taking every turn and movement with foreseen recognition
he knows the layout and the route to the front door without
a misstep.*

...They pass you by. Snub you, cross the street. Hold
their breath, press their kids tighter to their sides as if
they'll be snatched up, swallowed whole by the street itself.
It can happen though. It happens and until it does you
never know if this is your last night in a bed, at a dinner
table, in a warm shower with shampoo. Those little things,
the smell of perfume, steam of a warm bath, taste of fresh
fruit. Those little things...

*The boy in the box stumbles out the front door and
down the steps, almost taking a fall as one foot scuffs the
other. Regaining balance his pace picks up and he runs on
that crumbling concrete sidewalk.*

And the man rambles on.

...When you're on the street, there's no downtime, no
nothing, no de-stressor. It's dropping your pride, forgetting
your dignity and holding out that expression, that pitiful yet
somewhat scary expression you need to put out for that bit
of change you're asking for. You look clean, you speak well,
you ask the right people, you can show 'em, let 'em know
you're not trash but even then, you're still trash to them, ya

know? They may give you a few bucks, but it's for their own peace of mind, not you. They couldn't give two shits. Probably thinking you'll go out and waste it on booze, not that you need a sandwich, not that you're literally dying of dehydration and malnutrition. No, they'd keep that far from their mind and let you die, long as it's in the back alleys, behind a dumpster where they can't see. Behind a dumpster, unseen and unheard and in their world, you don't exist...

The tracking shot of the boy smash cuts to him standing in his neighbor's house. He is surrounded by teenagers and twenty-somethings. There is no smoke billowing, no drugs being used and there is neither loud music nor multicolored lighting. The party greets him with stares and slack-jaws, their mouths open but wordless, perhaps caught in curiosity by his sudden appearance during mid-conversation. They're silent, taking in the sight of a child out of place. He stands near the door and scans across the room at the perplexed partygoers before spinning around and running out the door where the box turns black.

From the dirty man in the whitewashed room comes a brief break from his nonsense, a hint of textbook wisdom.

...I may not look it, but I'm smart. Believe me. I read books, lots of 'em. Text books, too. From the library, where I'm allowed but looked down on and watched. I know lots, but mostly I know about death. I know death well. You know there are many stages? Death isn't simple. There's sociological death, that's when your friends, family and others aware of your presence in this place accept that you're about to die. Then there is psychological, when you yourself accept that you're dying. And then there's biological, which is pretty straight forward. The body dies...

From the blackness of the screen inside the corner box, the boy emerges. Running as fast as he can, huffing and puffing as his young lungs work themselves as hard as they can, weary of the ruined concrete of the sidewalk his legs make short strides yet they are nonetheless hasty in his state of panic.

...There are other stages, you've probably heard of 'em. The five stages, one is denial. Two is anger. Three is fear. Four is bargaining and five is acceptance and, they're all emotions. They say these are the emotional stages someone goes through when given a terminal diagnosis. I don't know, never known anyone that's been through that. I haven't myself. Could all be bullshit, hell, it could all be. Birth, life, death... could all be bullshit...

He is out of his neighborhood on the downtown streets in the night, passing closed shops and open bars when and where a young boy should not be. Passersby there are none but, beggars and bums sitting in archways and resting on benches, there are plenty. They give no acknowledgement to his presence. He turns down an alleyway and slows as he finds the far side of a dumpster, tears have begun to streak his face and he sits to hug his knees to his chest and tries to make sense of everything he has witnessed in these fleeting moments.

Sitting in the darkness, cold and numb he leans against a brick wall in the shadow of a dumpster in an alleyway. He is hidden from the world. He is hiding from his own world.

The dirty man concludes his narrative.

...Everything I told you, everything I tell you, remember it. Forget what you know. The closest to the truth you'll get is right here. No one is honest. Sex is an absurdity, you can't get an honest word, everyone lies. It's ridiculous, they're ridiculous and we're ridiculous. Drugs, they're a part of life and you can't escape it. You can't escape death either. And as for the street, it don't matter what your name is, what your bank account has in it, the street calls your name every night. Like death, it calls to you, waits for you and watches for you, for any little opportunity to come snatch you up from your self-induced immortality and show you what it is you've been living for, what you've been missing, what you'll never get back and never have. Turns you into something you never thought you could be. If it catches you young or you're truly weak it turns you into a monster. To fight off the others at first but then it creeps up further and you're nothing more than a true, real life monster doing what you never thought yourself able. Doing the work only a monster would do. Believe me, this I know. This, I know..."

For the first time since the room popped up, the man turns his head to the side and the view opens, expands and, like a camera pushing out slowly, a pool of blood enters the frame. A wrinkled hand, a freckled arm and then a bald head of a bearded man with chapped lips and brown teeth and jowls is in place on the otherwise clean, sterile white floor.

He is the dirty man's victim.

He was the dirty man's audience for the speech on sex, drugs, homelessness and death. An interpretation, the one-

man show a sort of self-justification for the taking of life. As he sits and watches the pool of blood grow wider, thicker, the box in the corner of the young boy replays itself in another random sequential order.

A visual picture-in-picture to play along with the narrator's personal account, his self-telling of the events in a way only a shattered mind could share. Two pieces of a puzzle, one piece connected and somewhat cohesive and the other a jumble of events that skip forward, backward and side to side, freeze and repeat in variations one no more authentic than the other. A mind's memory susceptible to being dubbed and exaggerated by traumatic events, should they have even happened.

In the small box in the corner, the boy runs...

A Secret Love

I had a girlfriend in the _____ grade. A secret girlfriend. I never told anyone about her. She was ____, ___ and named...

I loved her.

No one knew. We didn't talk in class or sit near one another, not even at lunch. I followed her home every day after school staying ___ houses behind, always ___ houses behind and I kept her pace. She lived ___ houses down from me, on the same side of the street. Practically neighbors.

Her front door would be closed by the time I passed by and she'd be watching me from the front window.

And that's how I knew...

She loved me, too.

NO X AND A BIG O

Look at her/him, isn't she/he precious? Such innocence. Such warmth. You're in love with her/him. She/he is nothing but purity. You're going to marry her/him, it's only a matter of time before you can't contain yourself and the words stutter out. But remember, if not you, someone had that lovely woman/man with her/his panties in her/his mouth to muffle the screams of pleasure, her/his wrists and ankles bound with velvet rope as she/he was blindfolded and punished in ways that only she/he could ask for.

For her/him, there is no special day to give that special demand to punish every special, sacred inch of skin. For her/him, every day is Valentine's Day.

THAT PINK HAIRED ONE

We are here in this place and though neither of us have a solid foundation... We are standing, she with grace and beauty and I with aspiration. A smile greets me with open arms and I'm brought in, warm and muddled by her charm. Her smile... it lures me, her eyes... they fill me, her touch... it binds me. There is a moment of silence as we separate, our bodies adjust and start anew, and though the night has just begun I am absorbed. She speaks, I listen, secretly wishing, that this encounter is no passing gesture. There is a sense within myself, an ache that cannot be identified or perhaps, is simply not familiar. I grow quixotic, bold, hoping not to nettle the semblance or chance misguidance. I'm bestowed and the air is soft, gentle, subtle... The night ends and as she departs I'm left with the taste of her, the smell of her, and the wonder of what this will become and, the hope that whatever this may have been, that it will carry forth, grow and strike a tune beyond this surreal purlieu.

I hear she cried. Her eyes melted, black tears smeared baby-doll skin. A picture is snapped, tattooed, printed on my brain. Hoping she can hear the thoughts, *shake it off, kid, shake it off.* I know the emoticon for which is adequate. Thinking of her, I write as I always do... always thinking of her, eyelid twitching to a beat without rhythm, closing to images, blinking flashes of light within the darkness: pink hair upon my chest, a playful bite to a cheek, a petite body warming me. Though she's hours away I can dream... It beckons me, the memory, the metaphors. *I miss her*, I say to myself knowing well it could hurt. Knowing well it's worth it all, everything and anything. A sudden realization, yet nonetheless than truth... *I miss her.* Tonight, last night, tomorrow night I want her *·I want her·* to cuddle, to kiss, to share a moment in this lifetime. Whether a moment of tears or laughter, of laughter and tears... a moment of this lifetime...

I wait in our room... The very same room of the last and the first secret rendezvous ··the purposely out·of·the·way, dirty, cheap, unknown motel in a purposely unknown, cheap, dirty, out·of·the·way small town·· I wait, alone, at a small table for her arrival. A book plays the role of companion. Chapters One and Two finished by the time notices comes via wireless voice command. They come in spurts, jumbled together or short, out of relation and erratic. The country service bars hit or miss, spiking in unexplainable random points. *Forty·five minutes* she says, *thirty minutes* she says, *forty·five minutes* she says and I wonder if she has become victim to a form of vortex or misplaced in another dimension on the lonely, plain and monotonous interstate. Hypnotized eyes unaware her German compact has passed the very same natural landmarks repeatedly... repeatedly... repeatedly... repeatedly... *Four hours, three hours, four hours* later I've finished the final chapter as knuckles rap upon the door to the room, *our* room... Through years of confined cigarette smoke that clogs pores of skin like sweat on a mid·August night, I can smell her perfume. It lures me.

Overtaken by immediate lustful elation clothes are shimmied up and down and aside other than removed and the bed linen remains folded and straight as we tumble... I, like a forlorn parolee and she, like a woman of the night. We slip from the edge of the mattress to the floor and I twist and wriggle, mounting her atop of me. The carpet brash against my exposed backside creates a burn as we thrust together. A stark pain grinds on as our pelvic bones meet, two small creatures bruising sensitive areas in part for sexual pleasure. That pink hair dangles as she allows her head to loll forward, the ends tickling my lower stomach below the t-shirt bunching beneath me. I thrust and wrap my arms around her, pulling her down to my chest and she continues to grind and swivel. Tight, strong, my muscles flex as I keep her face buried. Her voice is muffled and her nails dig into my shoulders, hands begin to claw at my face. I continue to thrust until I finish... Not aware that her flailing has ceased, her legs limp and hips stationary and, as I release her that beautiful face —now contorted in a shocking display of death-- slides to a *thump* against the floor.

We are in this place, *our* place... and I have just killed my secret lover in a remote location during what was to be -- for the better of both our professional lives-- a night's encounter kept hidden from all but the two of us artists. She, the figure of an actress and I, the shell of a screenwriter... we, the socially denied couple. This dreadful death an accident, deplorable, excruciating yet it urges my mind to wander to the form of an outlet. In the perspective of my mistress I live the intense closing moments as her neck is crushed and her brain denied blood and oxygen... a terrifying and unfortunately foreseen coming end of an all-too-brief onscreen life and a long series of hardships off-screen flash in like comic book panels. From birth to the darkness before the final "Cut," the final exhausted hollering of "That's a wrap!"

I'm daunted by the images and truth of the task that now lies at hand. The memory of her by fans, friends and family will be judged by the source of her death, accidently forced by a composition of hunger and passion it must not be known and must be countered by a mystery to keep suspicions abound. In a fury, I scribble the note that is to accompany her suicide, an outlet flooded and plugged by the end of a morbidly beautiful vignette. Amongst a heartfelt goodbye and a thank you to some, is a finger poking at the chest of one that broke her heart and drive to carry on.

Some days later I read she suffered with chronic depression: memories, the after effects of countless tragedies of a falling star struggling through life with no place to reach for relief or comfort other than in the arms of an affair with an undisclosed secret lover. A series of misfortunes that brought her to wits-end which happened to also be the end of a belt hanging in the closet of a dirty, small town motel room... her body swaying gently back and forth with the faint echo of delirious laughter in the room as reported by the undisclosed man, the secret lover and unknown co-perpetrator of this purposely out-of-the-way rendezvous.

We were there in that place and though neither of us had a solid foundation, we stood. I heard she cried, black tears smeared baby-doll skin and I waited in that room, *our* room... to be overtaken by immediate lustful elation and to read some days later that she took her life... that pink haired one... she took her life.

AND AFTERWARDS...

And afterwards...

I told her to name the baby after Elizabeth Taylor instead of Marilyn Monroe if it was a girl and, Montgomery Clift instead of James Dean if it was a boy.

She said, "Who are they?"

I told her to forget about it.

She said with a smile, "That's something for us to talk about," and watched me walk away.

As I left the store I saw her wave from her post at the dressing rooms and I waved back...

Scurrying off like a scared sewer rat.

...Soon, the Unknown

The drive is symbolic, a sentiment of a growth and passion: a distance, a change, perception and want creeping from the shadows of my being. Twilight inches along the walls as I fall into her...

My eyes melt upon her skin...

I listen and absorb her thoughts, she fills me and when I speak, I wish to be silent, to listen to her voice...

A voice that raises gooseflesh.

In a sense of secrecy, I wonder if this will not be a passing instance and then, an ache arises, unidentified or perhaps, until this moment...

Unknown.

Quixotic, bold, hoping not to nettle the semblance or give misguidance...

Soft and subtle and gentle, the night continues and as we...

Caress, I feel warm and I hope and wonder if this tune will ring out past this surreal purlieu or if...

If... I'm alone.

North Vermont and Lexington

"Ladies and gentlemen, we seem to be experiencing some slight turbulence and request that you return to your seat and buckle your seatbelt. Once we are clear the seatbelt light will be turned off and I'll make an announcement on our conditions. Thank you for your understanding." The light above my head turns on and there is a ding as the Captain's intercom is flicked off. I stare out the window and admire the lined countryside some thirty-three thousand feet below, dirt roads mapping small towns of the Midwest. The airplane jostles and I grasp my armrest, not out of fear but in seek of reassurance.

I am officially on my own; a fresh college graduate with a major in History and a minor in Philosophy on the forefront of induction into adulthood: the west coast, California, Los Angeles.

Though I cannot see her face, I know my mother is crying. She is not capable of controlling her emotions upon my departures, whether it be for a weekend to the grandparents or a semester to Plattsburgh University. Assumptions are plenty, but I truly cannot explain why she holds such emotions towards my presence or lack thereof. Possibly because I am her last to leave the den, her baby cub, but that is only one of said assumptions. Wrapped in my father's arms, she must feel comforted. Their marriage having survived all the years since the first born, there must be more than physical attraction and love within their relationship. They stand at the window together, father holding mother, he himself holding back tears as they watch my plane lift off and disappear into the clouds. They will wait far beyond the sight of the plane, frozen by the realization of the aspect that my life is about to confront; they having done the same as I in their day and they, too, having not known their inborn anxiousness and desires for this migration.

Staring at the specks of land as they pass between the white billows I muse over sporadic memories, as abrupt as my decision to travel west... *golden leaves caught in the wind, twirling through damp autumn nights... scavenging through textbooks for accomplishments of the Industrial Age... the look on my first girlfriend's face as she broke my heart... standing above the fresh dirt that covered my childhood pet and best friend, Thor... the stoic nods of comprehension my mother and father and older siblings gave in return to my attempts to verbally explain the feelings within me to compose this journey...*

My thoughts are interrupted by the ding of the Captain's intercom, followed by his voice, "Ladies and gentlemen, the turbulence seems to have cleared and you are now allowed to unbuckle and move about the cabin as you wish."

I stand and stretch, arching and folding my arms behind my back to crack sore bones. I roll my head and touch my toes and bend side to side. I slide a foot forward and raise my arms together, bracing my weight on my front leg and reach for the sun. "We're everywhere." Startled, I turn around. She's beautiful, short and curvaceous with dark hair, sharp, piercing eyes and light-caramel skin.

Noticing my confusion, she says, "Yogis, it's good to see people taking care of themselves." Nodding, I accept her hand in mine. "Andrea," her tone is petite and feminine. "And how about you? Do you have a name or are you some mysterious stranger to become a brief friend for the following duration of this flight?"

The wit of her words flatter her physical attraction and I attempt to speak but only mumbling escapes my mouth, "I... I'm, my name is..." She smiles, her perfect teeth shine between lips as ruby as a freshly plucked rose.

"That's okay, mystery man. Names aren't important here." She waves to her seat and the empty isle seat beside it, "Care to join me?"

"Ya-Yes, that would be nice." I'm caught off-guard by my own openness to join her without hesitation or thought. Andrea stands a few rows down and taps the headrest, gesturing for me to sit before moving herself in the row. I slide into the seat and through the corner of my eye I catch her stuffing a book into a backpack, the cover familiar. I nod, pointing at the book, "What's that?"

She retrieves the hardcover and sets it on her lap, gently dusting the jacket free of an unseen film, a soothing motion. "*A History of the Underground*," she says in a low voice, seemingly embarrassed by its presence. "I'm kind of a History nut... majored in it to be honest."

My eyes spark with an equal share of enthusiasm and curiosity, "Seriously? I recently earned my Bachelors in History." I lay out my hand, "May I?"

"Well, of course." Andrea, the sweet young History major raises the armrest and relaxes a knee on the seats and once suitably adjusted, passes me the book. "What a coincidence... *wow*... cute, in shape *and* educated." I glance over to meet her smile, which I return ·· a bit red-faced, as is she. "Are you familiar with the author?"

"Are you kidding?" a smile purses my lips. "Henry Bloomfield, today's most prominent author of counter-cultural history? Yes, I've read his work." I begin to laugh and she playfully slaps my shoulder.

"Did you read *Rituals of the Americans*?!"

My attention falls from the book and focuses on Andrea's face. "I've never been so fascinated! Hands down Bloomfield's best work."

"My thesis was heavily influenced by that book. It's utterly inspiring and robust." She brings both legs up to sit cross-legged, comfortably fitting her tiny frame on the confined seats.

I sit silent, staring not into her eyes but into her *being*, making a summation of her essence as though I have known her for countless years. "You have no idea how many sleepless nights this book caused me. No joke, this book caused my insomnia."

"I've read it three times."

"Four!"

She grabs me by the shoulders and shakes me back and forth. "I can't believe this!" she deadpans the excitement in her voice. "Who are you and what are you doing on this plane?" We share a moment, a pause, curious eyes staring into one another before we break into laughter and Andrea leans toward me and glances at the book between us. As her head dips I gain view through the window, the small towns are now replaced by generous green mountains.

My thoughts flutter... *summer nights rolling though the downtown streets on my bicycle... stuttering with my first written words on my mother's lap as we read together, the title long forgotten... my friends' unrecognizable scribbles on my arm cast when I was in fifth grade... the relief of the first dip into the Hudson river on the first day of summer vacation...*

She straightens up and her eyes wander into mine, "Are you okay, mystery man?" her voice sincere and genuine.

I sigh and nod.

Andrea's hands slide down my arms and take hold of my hands, "You're cold... *and* sweaty..."

I pull my mind from the daze, "Yes, sorry. I'm all right, just – just reminiscing."

Andrea bites the side of her lower lip, making a lively face. "Girlfriend?"

I blush. "No."

"Ex-girlfriend?"

"Nope."

She reads me with a squint and with her lip free from her teeth, says, "I know. Home... family, friends... childhood."

I'm taken by her sudden glimpse into my thoughts. "Yeah, exactly." I laugh nervously. "It's strange, I have been thinking about the past since I got on this plane. And before, up to today, all I could think of was the future, California. Then as I'm traveling there, to this land of sunshine and celluloid all I can think about is home."

Somehow this woman knows me, intimately it seems. Or maybe, it is not me she knows, maybe it is my situation. "I understand," she says and I believe her.

"Daydreaming..."

"I used to dream about California." She releases my hands, "I would be standing on the street watching the sunset and in that serene beauty, have this overwhelming feeling of anxiousness, hopelessness, just this... *feeling*. I don't know where it came from, that feeling. I probably never will."

"And now you're following your dreams –"

"No," she interrupts, "and now I'm following this inborn sensation that's been humming in the background like a furnace, until now, when it's about to burst!" Her chest rises and falls quickly and deeply as she catches her breath, "I'm sorry, I don't know what came over me, I just couldn't hold it in."

"I know," I say, with complete honesty. "The instinctive inner-self this culture feels tugging them from the insides... this unexplainable custom we all feel and feel the need to embrace yet don't have the ability to comprehend... I don't know, I just don't know..."

"You've had the dreams too," she says matter-of-fact. "I think we all have."

"Yes, I've had them."

She doesn't ask me nor do I ask her: *What is this passage and where is it bringing us and what does it mean? Or want?*

Time passes as we watch the earth move outside the window of the airplane, neither of us speaking. Lights flood the ever-darkening sky, greens and yellows and oranges. It's mesmerizing to watch as they pass in no particular order but in some matter, way back when, these lights had an order to them and there was a reason for their particular patterns. This I *know*.

The Captain's intercom dings and his voice crackles through the air, "Ladies and gentlemen, we are approaching our destination of Los Angeles, California. We ask you to please return to your seats and prepare for landing by buckling your seatbelts and stowing all bags under the seat in front of you or in the overhead compartments. And as always, we thank you for your business and hope you'll join us again soon."

As I rise to pardon myself Andrea grabs my arm, "It's nice to have met you, mystery man." Her lips form a weak smile and she drifts back to the window, releasing me.

I feel inclined to ask, "Isn't this your stop?"

"I feel it is," her gaze remains on the night outside, "but I don't want it to be."

***

I stand on the corner of North Vermont and Lexington, the sun falling between apartment buildings, casting shadows in alleyways and, within these last shimmering moments I feel the beginnings of an apathetic fog shroud my body... an anxiousness, a hopelessness.

ROUTINE

Watching from a second story window, I can't help but feel an odd sympathy for the young man below. He walks back and forth, from one edge of the sidewalk to the other, his head down, staring at his feet as they make their small, frenzied steps. The book-bag strapped tight on his back makes his naturally slouched posture appear evermore exaggerated. His hands fidget with one another, held out in front of his chest, twirling and intertwining and untwining. And as if he knows I'm watching, he stops moving and raises his head and finds my eyes with his own. They stare deep within me and seem to latch onto something within, I can feel their weight tugging inside of me and, for a brief moment before he looks away and continues his daily routine, I understand.

USED

-sniff

She was (only women leave that natural powder and flower scent that lingers behind all else) a smoker.

-sniff

She rolled her own cigarettes, non-filters.

She was older.

-sniff

Elderly.

Sanitation, a sterile sanitation.

The smell of cardboard.

-sniff

She was sad... in pain, perhaps both. Tear drops, crinkled dots upon the page blurring the text. Blood on the next...

A crimson smear. A droplet, an attempt to rub it away crinkled the page, the blood dark and lighter near the end where the fingers lifted.

-sniff

Death.

She died reading this book.

She...

An elderly woman died, a smoker's lungs filled with disease, years of meticulously rolled Buglers failed to be hidden by... pages turned, turned... turned.

-sniff

Perfume. A soft, seductive yet refined fragrance.

Hidden, hidden like this book from prying eyes (embarrassment perhaps by its content) in a shoebox.

She cried as she read, her pain or sadness and/or both on the pages.

A memory of youth as the blood, coughed up on the page, smeared, seized her frail body.

-sniff

The book clenched to her chest in a final embrace, a final cough, a final breath and clenched until... pages turned, turned... turned.

-sniff

A man (the scent of musk that only men possess) donated the book, this book to thrift.

Discarded and alive once more -- to tell a story beyond those of the pages.

SAND BUCKET

Well, I suppose I'd like to thank you all for coming. It means a lot to my wife and I and, I know it means a lot to Chris. I can't describe to you how it feels standing up here so I guess I won't try. I'm assuming you all understand if I'm a little off this morning, he was a good boy. Different, no doubt different, but a good person... his own person, but no doubt different no one can argue that. I'm supposed to be up here to tell you about my boy, about his life, how proud of him I am and how much I love him, how he'll be missed. But I can't do that, it wouldn't be right and he wouldn't want that no matter how much I fight with myself to keep the pride and praise down. When Chris came along, we struggled, my wife and I. Hell, did we ever struggle. We tried, we pleaded, cried, scolded... everything we thought we should do to raise him right we did. To see that he had a decent upbringing and teach him the basics for the foundation of life... it didn't turn out that way did it? No. He didn't learn how we thought he should, he didn't want to learn any way but his own and now, as we're struggling with his passing, we're learning that we weren't the teachers. That he in fact taught us. I got here something I wrote down last night. It's about Chris, about us, his family and about how he began to show us who he was. It may be a little long, or a little short and probably a little strange but please... bear with me.

Chris was eight-years-old when we took him upstate for a few weeks near the end of August. He loved the beach, the sand, the water, the rocks, everything about it. On our last day he threw a fit, he wanted to see the beach once more before we left. So, we gave in and drove over. We watched him from our blanket, he waded in the water and built himself a castle. He sat next to it as the tide came in and tore it down, wave by wave, just sitting there watching it erode. And then when we called to him, that it was time to go, he stood and stared out over the water as if there was a ship there, but there was none and when I called for him again, he scooped some sand into his little plastic bucket and slowly made his way up the beach to his mother and I.

We let him keep it, the sand. By then we knew he was a little different, we just didn't know how much so. Some kids collect shells, some rocks or even bugs, butterflies. I thought maybe he decided to bring some sand home as a keepsake. He carried that bucket of sand with him everywhere he went, taking care of it as a mother would her newborn. It was at the dinner table; he even gave it its own spot with a plate and silverware and glass. It was in the backyard, in his wagon and, he even brought it to bed with him. We humored it of course, for a while. As we spoke one night in bed, talking about how we would have to break this odd behavior before school started, we heard a voice.

It was Chris.

The first time we had heard our son speak was through the bedroom walls as he tucked in his friend, his best friend, his only friend... that bucket of sand. It's as though he knew what we were planning to do and he couldn't let us split him up from his best friend. And we couldn't. Neither I nor his mother had the heart after hearing him speak. It was a moment, I'll tell you, a true heartwarming moment that reminds you of why you have children in the first place.

School started a week or two after that night. We got calls, oh yes did we get calls, plenty of them. From the teachers, the principal and even his classmates' parents trying to give us some friendly advice, parent to parent. I don't blame them, no, they saw him get teased and bullied and, I can't say I wouldn't have done it different if I were them. But wouldn't you know it, the more we heard about having to change things, the more we saw him bond. The more we felt like the bad guys when we tried. When you learn of your child's true enjoyment in life, you don't take it away. Even if you do, you can't keep it away. That's not right. And one night, after a conference with his teacher we were convinced that the separation must take place for him to flourish, to be... a normal little boy. That teacher had our son's best intentions in mind, but she was wrong, we were wrong. That night I tried to lecture him, I told him how he was growing up and growing up meant making changes, giving up childish things. And when he didn't see it that way I tried to bargain with him. And when that didn't work, I got angry. To this day I wish I could go back and go about that night differently. But I can't and I have learned to live with it and I will continue to.

As he had begun talking to that bucket of sand, they had conversations, innocent conversations, he talking to the bucket and answering as though it talked right back to him. And maybe it did, who is to say it didn't? We, all of us had imaginary friends. His, well his was just plastic and though that scared us, we still shouldn't have taken it from him. I took that bucket from my crying son and just as I was about to dump it over the porch railing, my wife, Chris' mother, that beautiful lovely woman with her soft voice, she placed a gentle hand on my shoulder and asked me to do something I'm ever so grateful she asked.

The following days played out like weeks, months even. When we'd see him off at the school bus, he wasn't respondent. Reports came home that he seemed very depressed, lonely. When he came home, he'd go to his room and sit on his bed, he wouldn't move until dinner and then he wouldn't eat. He'd go straight back to his room after and sit there again until we tucked him in. Every night, we'd hold back our tears as he stared off into the darkness and we said goodnight, wishing, praying that he would talk, which he hadn't done since I took that bucket from him. I'm not a religious man, never have been, my wife neither, but we prayed, we prayed to whoever or whatever could be listening for the slightest muttering, a single word from our son.

It broke our hearts. I know it broke mine. Every day, every morning and every night our hearts were torn apart. It killed me to see him like that, a shell of a boy.

I don't know how long it took for us to realize our mistake, but when he saw me coming towards him with that bucket still filled with that sand from the beach, he smiled. A smile so big and genuine I'll never forget it; I'll never need a picture because it's imprinted on the back of my eyelids. He took that bucket and ran, he ran down the stairs and before he got to the door, he turned back around and ran to me. From where he stood on the stairs, with me a step above him, he wrapped his hands and arms around my legs and squeezed tighter than any hug I'd ever felt. The bucket swayed and hit the back of my legs as he held it there, his hands twined together around me. I held him there as long as I could only letting him go when I could feel the eagerness eating away at him. He ran back down those stairs and out the door into the backyard and he stayed there, chatting away with his friend and digging in the dirt with his trucks. Playing out all the scenarios the quote "normal little boys" end quote would play, right there in the dirt. The only difference is his best friend, his only friend and perhaps as I read this, I think maybe even a part of himself, being that bucket of sand.

The teachers called again, the principal too. The other parents seemed to ignore it now, our boy being beyond help in their view I suppose. He came home roughed up, bloody nose here and there, ripped clothing, messed hair, but he was always smiling and as long as he was smiling we knew he was happy and that's all that mattered. As long as he was happy, he could set a place at our table for that bucket of his for the rest of his life if he wanted. He was happy, and that made us happy.

As summer approached we planned our next vacation, and though at the time to him it may have seemed like the world, we were going upstate to the lake again. It didn't feel good, I can tell you that with complete honesty, thinking that I was in some way letting him down by not having the money for any extravagance that he may have heard of from the other kids bragging about their summers as kids do, but his face lit up when we told him we were going back to the lake, that was all the notice I needed to know I had done something right. When his schoolmates were going to amusement parks and warmer climates, camps and Disneyland, he was happy to play in the wet sand on a beach at the lake.

School was about to end for the year and though Chris should have been all smiles, he began to show signs of a sadness, one that seemed to have been awakened the morning after we first told him about returning to the lake. It crept up, growing more prominent by each day. We didn't understand. He had his bucket, he had the sand, he had it with him twenty-four hours a day, seven days a week. But there was a difference and that difference grew. They didn't speak as often and, when they did there wasn't that spark or peak of excitement that there was before. When they played, the bucket became more and more of an observer. It went from being tucked in bed with him to sleeping on the floor next to him and eventually, at his feet at the dinner table.

The day we left for the lake there seemed to be almost no anticipation coming from the back seat and what struck me, what really sticks in my mind, is unlike all the other car rides, the bucket wasn't strapped in its seatbelt beside him but was on the floor, where it could easily fall over with an abrupt turn or braking. The disregard and silence bothered my wife and I, we both sat with a fake calm and though we cheerfully talked about the next two weeks to come, smiles on our face, they were forced. She never said so, but I know hers were as long and blank as mine. I know now, that the car ride was a sign of things to come.

Over the two weeks we spent the days like what we had come to accept we would not be: a normal everyday family. We strolled up and down the main street stopping in shops, we bought hats with whistles attached, shirts with the name Lake George printed on it... we played miniature golf, dropped quarters in video games and ate pizza for dinner and stopped in the candy stores for dessert. We tried, if there is a lord he or it knows we tried. But Chris just wasn't happy and all we could think of was to call it an early onslaught of teenage angst towards all things as ridiculous as that sounds. Things like parents, friends, himself and life in general but we knew this wasn't the cause, a boy that age doesn't have angst. At least that's what we thought in our hearts and in our hearts we were dying, slowly, watching our son in his dismay.

I remember vividly the night on the dock, holding him up, making remark on how much more he weighed than the last time I lifted him, how much more he had grown. It had been too long since I had last held my boy in the air. I held him up so he could scan the lake and the mountain range on the other side through one of those timed binoculars you pump quarters into. As the time ticked down I told him how we were leaving the next morning and that if he wanted to, we could stop by the beach one last time before heading home, like we had the year before. The time went up and the binoculars clicked black and I set him on his feet... that's when I noticed. I don't know how I hadn't noticed this earlier, but that is when I saw that he did not carry the sand bucket. It wasn't dangling from his hand, arm swaying back and forth gingerly in that perky little step children have when they're content and unaware of the world around them, completely satisfied by their own and their own only. How I envy them for being able to do that, sometimes I wish

I could join them in their little worlds they have... But, when I asked him about the beach, he nodded and wandered down the dock, away from his father, from his mother. When we returned that night to the hotel, I saw that he had placed the bucket on the bedside stand. It had been there the whole day and I had not known until that moment we shared on the dock.

The next morning, we went to the beach, Chris had his bucket and before we had our blanket on the sand he was down at the waterline and... what he did then I couldn't believe.

He dumped the sand out.

It could have been from where he first dug it up, that point exactly, I didn't know. I still don't. When he tapped the bottom of the overturned bucket, satisfied it was empty, he turned and began up the beach toward us, a quick stride to his step and a small smile on his face. My wife, how beautiful she looks today, as beautiful as she looked that very day, put her arm around me and rested her head on my shoulder. We spent the rest of the morning together as a family, on that blanket reading and watching other vacationers pass. When he fell asleep between us, me staring at the open water and she reading one of her paperback novels, we decided it was time to pack up.

The car was almost set, all that was needed was Chris and the blanket we allowed him to continue to sleep on as we packed the items we brought on the beach with us.

I stood at the car and watched as the mother of my child shook our boy awake, gently, as gentle as the hand she placed on my shoulder that night on the porch. He rubbed his eyes and she told him it was time to go, I couldn't hear her voice but I could see her lips move. He came to the car, his hand in her hand, the blanket rolled up under her other arm. She smiled at me with the pride and love only a mother, a wife, a lover could smile and when they made it to the car, he freed his hand and in one quick movement, reached into the backseat and grabbed that bucket and began to run down the beach as fast as his little legs would take him.

We watched as he stood at the water, the waves licking his toes and we gave him a minute to say goodbye. Allow him to say goodbye in his way, as we believed he was doing. Like how one says goodbye to a lifelong friend or family, as I'm doing now. I called to him and he turned to come, took a step and stopped. He bent down and scooped that bucket halfway full of wet beach sand. The smile he wore as he walked back up to the car made my own that much brighter.

I don't expect you to put much into this story, but to me and to my dear grieving wife, it is the story of our boy taken away from us all too soon. Our boy, unlike any other who has ever walked this earth, who had become his own person at such a young age and taught not just his mother and father what it meant... what it meant to be yourself, to create and be yourself no matter how much pressure you feel. He taught us not just that, but taught us to create our own happiness and showed us all here today just how special each and every story that makes up the body of our lives are.

FOR HER, INSOMNIA

She grasps my hand as I point the remote towards the television and says, "I can't sleep without the noise." I free my hand and snuggle close to hold her beautiful nude body and kiss her neck. And as I close my eyes for a sleepless night I can't help but wonder what demons await her in the silence.

WINTER IN SEASON

"It's snowing," she says. I peer out the window and agree. "What shall we do now?" Shaking my head I gesture indecision with a rise of my shoulders. "Sleep it off?" she suggests. Nodding, I crawl into bed and reach for her. "Cold hands!" she shivers at my touch. I let go, she rolls away, and I accept that winter has come in season, in body and in mind.

It Rained

Time couldn't heal...

I can't be certain what time or even what day, but it was late. And it was late winter. The night was frigid, the air chilled bone. The snow buried the sidewalk, hiding the ice from eyes. Soft, white powder that children dream of until adulthood, when winter weather becomes a burden instead of a sight of wonder.

Pool was the game and the game was good. One-Pocket played solo. Not much action upstate on a downtown weeknight. I played a few racks, the stick warped and the balls dull of color, numbers half erased. If not for what little color remained the balls wouldn't have had any source of identification besides round and hard. Round may not even be proper as years of abuse left them chipped. It matched though. It matched the table, the once light-green felt torn in places and darkened with stains.

Well, I played a few games, bought a bottle of beer and kept my corner of the place clean. My thick jacket on a tall stool, mirrors reflecting an empty bar sans the bartender and myself, who watched me play with outstretched palms resting on the bar. When I'd break for a sip of Arrogant Bastard Ale, I'd think about asking him to join but reasoned he would have invited himself had he wished. I put a five-dollar bill in a tip glass when I left, feeling as though if I hadn't been there he would have closed up the place.

The bar was on a corner and as I exited, turning the corner to the parking lot adjacent I met her, walked right into one another as I fumbled with my jacket's zipper. She almost fell but we grabbed at each other quickly and I kept her up... on her feet...

I kept her on her feet...

She wiggled a little, sort of a funny looking dance trying to keep her balance. She steadied herself with my assistance and once again I found myself fumbling, this time with my words. Though my thoughts flowed freely, I could not release them verbally. I meant to say, "Excuse me, I'm so sorry it was entirely my fault I should have been looking where I was walking." But I couldn't. I stared blankly at her beautiful, flirtatious smile. And those words stayed trapped inside my mind, floating... floating past my eyes like a cartoon yet I unable to voice them... they kept my mouth open like an awestruck child. I would have caught flies if it had been a winter's cousin.

Before she spoke, before I knew her name, before I kissed her lips, before I smelled her hair... I was in love. That really happened, you know. No question about it. People fell in love at first sight and I knew then she was going to be mine.

It was she that broke the silence. She apologized and I mumbled something I can't remember, likely because it made no sense. It was like that for the first few dates. She talking and I listening, taking in every word, every breath but unable to express properly the emotions that I felt. Perhaps I was too shy, perhaps I was worried, perhaps even scared... scared that if I spoke up she would take those words and twist them in her own way, contort them into words I had heard in the past. She didn't. Not that I know of. When I began to feel comfortable those trapped thoughts escaped and I spoke up.

I wrote to her. Told her of my undying love, of every eyelash I watched twitch as she slept on my chest. And she wrote back likewise and this made me... happy. Something I had not been for a time I could not remember. You see, I had health troubles but I'll get to that soon. She spoke to me with love and that was the world to me, so much so that every once in a while I'd have to press myself against her as tight as I could, wrap my arms around her and squeeze to know she was real and not some solipsistic sentiment.

I mentioned troubles. I'll lay them out. I'd been ill for a long time. A serious illness I'd rather not get that in-depth about concerning its symptoms but in between what the doctors called "Flare-ups" and while in "Remission" I was attending college and learned something that I can use here which I find... odd, for lack of a better expression. I'd never used anything I never taught myself in the real world. But here is a first... like her.

I had this illness, I'd get dreadfully sick and a few years into the attacks I lost too much blood in one night and was rushed to the hospital. I was there for nine months, two surgeries, three times told I wasn't going to make it, told to become religious. I died three times. That's the truth. Three times I died and came back. And here is that college education I paid for...

There was more to death than just dying. *Click, bang, dead.* No, there was more. There were stages and the most important was biological death. You see, the body could quit but it may have also been forced to quit. Sometimes it could shut down trying to repair itself over a long period of time, cells replicated and tissues and organs worked overtime to stay functional or to remove foreign entities that affected proper operations until finally, the rate at which repair happened was overtaken by the rate at which degradation happened. So, the body gave up. Cells died, organs failed and the last breath ·· long and drawn out after an extensive fight·· exhaled and escaped. But it was different when the body was forced to shut down.

That final breath was often disguised as the final moment of life but that wasn't quite so. It was more complicated than that. It was cellular. Cells, those tiny bits that we took for granted, those little powerhouses that worked to hold us together by glomming together and forming tissue and organs and our system... Cells created life, built the organism's anatomy, dictated its physiology and facilitated its metabolism.

Yes, oxygen enabled life... air was brought into the lungs and transferred to the blood, gas exchanged creating a form of oxygen that a blood cell could carry and this dissolution into the blood created circulation ·· a beating heart and pumping blood line but metabolism, that's where the work happened.

It was death of metabolism, cellular respiration that depleted the body of its will to live by failing to create the food cells needed to do their jobs. When cells stopped working, stopped breaking down nutrients, stopped creating molecules, stopped recycling waste we stopped living. That last breath would eventually be used up, the last bits of oxygen squeezed into the blood to circle the body those last few times and perform the last few metabolic processes but what caused the last breath, why the body was dying in the first place was due to cells. They held the materials for the blood to dissolve oxygen and converted food to energy but what was even more rudimentary, even more microscopic and even more vital to life as an organism was what the cells contained deep inside their nuclei.

DNA, genetic material. Deoxyribonucleic acid dictated the cellular makeup of everything. Formed the chromosomes that created the genome, the entire collection of genetic information, instructions and the roadmap to organism creation. To have been useful it must have been replicated and therein lied the eventual problem: replication. A cell had a supply of genetic information that could only be replicated so many times and there were these... things, these buffer regions of unnecessary DNA sequences on the ends of chromosomes that protected the genes from becoming damaged and with each replication, see... chromosomes became shorter. Pieces became lost or damaged or jumbled and that's where telomeres hung out on the ends to make sure the important things remained safe and usable.

When the chromosomes became unusable, organism deterioration began and depending on the importance of the gene that had been damaged... Well, telomeres helped resist aging, cell death, and organism death.

If only telomeres had been infinitely long then perhaps we would have been able to produce infinite replications meaning, perhaps: eternal life. But that was not the case and we slowly aged and died as our cells lost their battle against deterioration.

Foregoing the body's drawn-out struggle to find equilibrium and surmount systemic death which it was constantly doing, even when healthy.

When death occurred abruptly the struggle became amplified and chaos ensued. Comparatively, natural death, even in the terminally ill, could've been perhaps considered calm.

Three times I experienced the brink, the edge, the last branch, root dangling off the side of the cliff of biological death. I went out into the darkness three times. No whiteness, no light, no tunnel, no floating or hovering, nothing. And when I came back I knew none of that mattered, because I was there and I knew that when it was my turn to leave, that was it. That was accepted. The rate of repair simply couldn't keep up, organs and tissues failed to remain functional and, click, bang, dead. Eased into death by a calmness formulated by narcotic IV drips all the while dreaming of infinite telomeres.

The only thing that played with me, got to me was that there on my last thread I had no one and I had nothing.

And until that night I ran into her, I hadn't known for what or why I clung to a seemingly meaningless life. A speck, a grain of sand on a beach my existence was in that world and then with that clumsy dance of misplaced balance and bodies colliding, I found it: my reason, my reasons, for each moment with her a reason why I held on. Each kiss, quiver of lips on skin, flesh meeting flesh, fingers entwined, each smile and laugh and lustful "I love you" stored away in the recesses to be pulled out on rainy days, part the clouds and brighten the sky. Every moment with her was a reason I never achieved biological death.

"Time heals all wounds..."

You'd hear that and see that everywhere you looked, people said it without knowing the meaning of the words or even caring for the meaning of the words to support those being presented to... They were just hollow sounds forming an abused phrase.

Time.

Heals.

All.

Wounds.

Bullshit.

Time healed nothing. Had you ever heard an inmate serving a life sentence speak those words concerning his own mental or physical state of being? *No*, and neither had I.

Once I was mentally prepared to express the true and full contents of my heart in every way humanly possible, as much as any sentient being could for an absolute being without growing into the quintessential godlike status I wished I could be for her, it ended. She could not accept the... the, profusion of absolute and total admiration, she could not return the outpour of devotion. She could not accept the eventual breakdown of the human organism and she could not accept the abrupt displacement or calm embrace of biological departure.

I knew without chance of expression that she did not share those sentiments in such extremes and perhaps, could not.

She left me and I was again on my own and life seemed meaningless. Yet I held an ounce of hope that time would heal the wound, that time would bring her back to me.

But before time could continue in my favor, in our favor...

It rained.

It came down like iron over Laos. Turned everything and everyone to crumbs and spread like pollen to catch in the gusts of millions upon millions of dustbowl winds before the sun lost its shine millions upon millions of years later. The star we picked out all those years before to be our star -- our star when not next to one another to look up to the night sky and know that she was looking up, thinking of me or I looking up thinking of her-- fizzled out, fizzled out and shut down all dependent life, all those planets dead, circling a burnt out disc as they grew farther and further away from a gravitational tug to wander their own paths into the dark abyss of space.

Time is what she needed.

Time is what we needed.

But perhaps somewhere in space a new explosion will burst forth with creation and like motes of pollen caught in a gust of wind they will one day drift to the ground to be buried and once again, surface to sprout life and, perhaps I will be among them and she will replace one of them and until then we are here and there, somewhere in some place. I alone without her as she wanders the absence of embodiment and perhaps when and if that one moment comes, we will be given a chance to forgo the shackles and confinement of a human body and experience existence as one true devotion.

TEMPER, RED AS HER LIPS

In her attempts to decode his vocalizations she turns a wrong corner and heads down a one-way street. Distracted, infuriated, regard is tossed out the window to settle amongst disbanded cigarette butts -- mutual friends in theory though blatantly unsuspecting in appearance. Screaming women stuck in golden era cardigans lift children into their arms and sprint for the sidewalk, escaping the danger within the street by mere moments. She stomps on the gas, gunning for an unseen victim, a hit-and-run on a purely anthropomorphic basis. A premeditated murder due to faulty foundations via instructions in a foreign language, misunderstood and guided by illustrations. Lost in her fervor the oncoming car is unseen and collides with a mighty force, crunching metal and shattering glass. She stumbles from the crash confused but unharmed, undaunted by the wail of the horn under the head of the departed innocence.

Determined to right what has not been wronged.

UNDER THE OVERPASS

I idle, coast forward, staring down the dilemma ahead and there is an overwhelming eagerness to be past this situation... as every time before. I ready myself through deep breathing and then...

I nod at the observers and rev the engine, letting them know it's on.

Applying the clutch and popping the stick into first gear I stomp the gas pedal, pop into second gear and then third gear. At sixty miles-per-hour I zig and zag around the bodies hitting the ground in front of me. I hit sixty-five miles per hour as I enter the momentary cover under of the overpass, the jumpers above rushing to the other side and at seventy miles-per-hour I again zig and zag around the bodies as they jump and fall from above. I make it through the gauntlet intact and unmarked, excelling down the freeway until, I come to the next overpass.

TRAVELIN MAN

My home city has seen its share of eccentric hobos, from bus stop philosophers, grocery store cart-pushin bottle collectors and neck-braced, Velco-shoed winos but the fellow this story is about is the most unique.

He went unnoticed at first, just another travelin man, passin though town, possibly wanderin away from the Greyhound station and likin' what he saw in our city and decidin to stick around for some time. Where he found that old milk-crate, who the hell knows, maybe he brought it with him. No one saw him comin into town and no one saw him set up on the corner. It isn't even known when he began to preach from atop that crate. But after some time, maybe a week or two, the locals began callin him the Travelin Man. I guess we'd all run out of original names for our colorful hobos. He didn't make much of a stir, he wasn't loud and he wasn't offensive at the start. Hell, before he came to be here he may not have even been homeless. The only reason we assumed he was homeless this time was because as the days went by his suit became weathered, his face went from clean shaven to bearded and his odor became strong as cat piss. He was seen in the mornin, afternoon, evenin and late at night. It appeared that he never left the top of that milk-crate.

When I say he preached, I don't mean preachin the bible or anythin like that. I mean preachin like one of those end of times nuts, though I guess they're in the bible mix so that doesn't sum it up too well. He would talk and talk, to anyone who had the gull to lock eyes with him or anyone who passed him at that, sometimes even to himself as smokers witnessed from outside the bars down the street out for a drag and a puff between beers. Why he was never arrested I don't know, if it had been me up on that milk-crate I sure as hell would have been brought in. They seemed to like lockin me up back then, when I drank. But on back to the preachin, it was about things to come, bad things, horrible things and they were goin to happen to everyone. What also caught some observant people, was that these events were all going to happen here, in this one small city, not worldwide or even county wide or state wide, but here, in Glens Falls of New York state.

When I saw him for myself, he was talkin almost intellectually, using words a scholar of American Literature might use when tired. His doomsday events were ridiculous of course, but he rambled on and on, as though he didn't need to breathe. I recall his words in my own, they don't have the flare or awe his did, but my memory will have to do in this case. He said a rain was goin to fall and a day or two into the constant pour, the water would turn black and look more like oil than rain. The puddles would merge into large pools, it would drip from gutters and roofs and surge its way to the nearest puddle and once large enough, that puddle would find another puddle and another and create a pool. These pools would defy gravity and build themselves into creations of liquid life, giant beings of thick, oily liquid. Some fifteen feet high, as tall as a one story buildin and they would bring chaos with them. Destroyin everythin in sight, killin anyone in their reach and impervious to any of our means of defense. As beings made of liquid, bullets would pass through, as would cars. Bombs would splatter the beings about their surroundings, but they'd only reassemble. And when it seemed that this citywide destruction would escalate and overrun nearby towns and cities and continue on elsewhere, it would stop. One day, the rain would stop, the dark, oily beings would fall to the ground and seep into the dirt and into the gutters and drainage pipes. When those who survived would go on to tell the tale to the world, they would find that no other population had seen such things, that they were alone in this horrific tale and it would go down as a legend of unexplained phenomenon. Eventually the federal government would investigate and would leave as they came, with reports and photos of the dead and devastation and no formal theory. And this is where the story ended, for me at least. As my one and only time in the presence of the Travelin Man was short, too short. And, as you know because I'm writin this, I should have listened. We all should have listened.

As the weeks past, the man's presence became an obscenity to those who took community pride to heart and beatings befell the Travelin Man. Men and women would argue, leading to a shoutin match and that would lead to the man being pulled from his milk-crate and punched, kicked and even choked until more reasonable citizens would interject and stop the assault. Sometimes the police would come, though it seemed they didn't have the wellbein of the preacher on the forefront of their minds and would leave him be as they found him, cut and bleeding instead of bringin him to the hospital or callin an EMT unit to be checked out. But battered as he was, he'd step right back up on that crate of his and begin right from the start, repeatin his tale and goin on and on with it. By the end, it seemed as though he was startin to plead less than preach.

He was at it for about a month and a half, and his disappearance is still in the air. No one really knows what happened but there are of course, those who swear they saw him dragged from his roost and stomped, tossed into the back of a pickup where a group of men tied him up and drove off. From that, most presumed he'd been tied up and killed, left out in the woods somewhere for animals to nibble on. There was no official search, as there was no official man... just a wanderin ghost in a human shell who stood on a milk-crate for six weeks and then disappeared. I don't know if I believe the whole pickup truck gang abduction, but I do know that he was gone the day I went to see for my own curiosity. As like some others, I don't have much of an educated hypothesis concernin the whereabouts of the Travelin Man, but there have been plenty of guesses that went through my mind. From him up and leavin on his own two feet, takin his crate with him, to bein hauled to jail, to the pickup truck abduction and hell, for all I know he could be in a rehab center dryin out. Though what I and the rest of the city do know, is that one rainy day, as we sat silently nervous, tryin to look as though we didn't believe his words, the rain did in fact turn dark and oily, and it did merge and those liquid creatures came and tore the city apart and killed hundreds of people. And then as suddenly as it started, it stopped. Everythin and more happened that he preached from his stoop.

The thing that really gets me, that really makes me wish I had stayed there on that corner a bit longer, maybe even politely conversed with the man, is what happened to that high school boy on the day the man supposedly left. How the kid had just up and disappeared, no explanation to his possible whereabouts, no leads. He simply vanished, *poof* and gone and, his face turned into posters on telephone poles and left for speculation among those who noticed. I know what you're thinking, that this teenage, high school kid was the Travelin Man who had not come from another town but actually the future, which I guess would make him the Time Travelin Man, and I'm not goin to argue that, what I'm goin to do is not argue nor am I goin to agree. Because when you've seen and witnessed what I've seen and witnessed, there isn't a thing that's a sure thing in our world and those worlds that surround it.

I sit some nights and stare out the window, watch the dark sky, the moon drift across the sky and I don't wonder when or if that rain is goin to come back. I don't wonder if another travelin man will wander into town. I wonder who will stand beside me and listen to every goddamn word he says.

VIRGIN BIRTH

It screams, arms flailing and legs kicking.

She stands over it, her shadow casting oblong across the crib.

She cries, tears streaking her cheeks.

"...know him as the Dweller in Darkness..."

It screams. Its mouth toothless and disfigured into a permanent scowl.

"...summoned to Earth's surface..."

Its arms calm, settle upon its chest.

"...he has come ravening to bring terror..."

Its legs jerk and slowly settle.

"...and destruction..."

It closes its black eyes. Its eyelids shut from the sides, fluttering as its screams hush to whimpers.

"...hidden foulness..."

A long, forked tongue juts out quickly then slips back between leathered lips.

"...where he dwelleth..."

She closes the book and wipes away her tears.

Its misshapen head lolls to the side and its breathing becomes heavy.

A shadow grows beside her, that of a man. Who puts a hand on her shoulder and to his question, she answers, "For now it is... for now."

SADOMASOCHISTIC MAN

Drug addicted, alcoholic, Sadomasochistic Man worships Satan and syringes.

A collector of hopeless, helpless, hapless flesh he loves injecting narcotics into caged rats; homeless youth...

With whom he invents games of tribute and worship to the gods of Drugs and Perversion.

THE SECRETS OF DR. SORTELLI

It was 1893 and the city of Chicago was center stage as the *World's Fair: Columbian Exposition* drew millions of visitors from around the globe to wander the streets of *The White City* to be dazzled by the demonstrations of technology and entertained by the amusements. Nikola Tesla was on hand to provide his alternating currents which lit up the entirety of the fair. His high-frequency, high-voltage source, generated by two-phase induction motors provided brighter and cheaper illumination than his rival and nemesis. Curious viewers were treated to exhibitions of the eccentric inventor's work in electricity, the most incredible of which was a performance by Tesla himself who shot lightening from the tips of his fingers.

The very first Ferris Wheel was the main draw of the midway (which itself was birthed and coined at the *Exposition* by an ingenious promoter), at 260-feet-high, it held sixty passengers in over thirty cars. From the vision of photographer Eadweard Muybridge, the first moving pictures were presented. The Zoopraxiscope, a glass disk imprinted with images that rotated, bringing the illusion of movement and motion. This device was an inspiration and forbearer to the Kinetoscope and the common motion picture film. Another outstanding presentation was that of the *Viking*, an exact replica of the Viking ship known as the *Gokstad*. The ship was built in Norway and sailed from its homeland to the *Exposition* via the Atlantic Ocean, Hudson River, Eerie Canal and the Great Lakes. But, even the most luxurious and famous of the fair's exhibitions and inventions couldn't contend with one particular outfit.

The particular outfit in question being that of *Buffalo Bill's Wild West and Congress of Rough Riders of the World*. Or, as it was more commonly known: *Buffalo Bill's Wild West Show*. Though not granted inclusion by organizers, Buffalo Bill set up outside the fair grounds and ran through the entirety of the six-months. The show had many events displaying popular western stars with skilled notables Frank Butler, Annie Oakley and Native American holy man and war chief Sitting Bull of the Lakota Sioux. Events ranged from sideshows, races, trick shooting and trick riding to the more elaborate such as the reenactment of the *Pony Express*, stagecoach robberies on horseback and an Indian attack on settlers thwarted by a cowboy posse lead by the star attraction and creator, Buffalo Bill.

The end of this cabin raid finale is where our story of prosperous railroad magnate Mr. Darrion Richmond and that of Dr. Sortelli begins.

Having traveled from his home in the affluent section of Utica, New York, Mr. Richmond, ··who saw himself as a cowboy of sorts at heart·· suffering from the weight of the 1893 Panic upon his chest and the death of his wife, Evelyn the year prior upon his conscious took to a visit of the Windy City. Not for the fair, but for his fascination with western life that was portrayed in *Buffalo Bill's Wild West Show* in hopes that the travel and show would re-stimulate his progress through life's travails.

Having marveled at the city's rebirth from the great fire during the ride in, the elder gentleman estimated a stroll through the south side after the show's conclusion would be a refreshing end to a wondrous day. Not a half-mile into his walk did a sudden stark pain strike his chest, a pain that of late had grown familiar and his pace slowed, each breath pushed harder until he came to lean against the stoop of a brownstone. Clenching his chest he balanced himself upon the brick when a call came from above.

"Excuse me, Sir. Are you all right?" asked the younger gentleman, Dr. Sortelli, peering down from a second story window.

Mr. Richmond inhaled deeply in order to reply, exhaling as he spoke. "I feel as though my heart should fail me at any moment."

"Do not move, I will be directly down to assist you. I am a doctor of medicines."

Before the elder could respond, the younger man was gone from the window and a moment later appeared on the steps of the building. "Please, come with me." Dr. Sortelli gently guided Mr. Richmond by the arm, up the steps and through the door of the brownstone.

"Sir, I don't believe I can make these -" Mr. Richmond began as he eyed the stairwell for the second floor.

Dr. Sortelli cut him off mid-sentence. "You will rest then, here," the younger man walked the elder to a single wooden chair resting against the wall of the open and empty front room. "Now, slow your breathing and rest here while I remedy you a tonic that will surely bring some relief to your ill."

The elder man gave a surprising and brief laugh. "Good Sir that you are, I appreciate your help but forgive me if I am skeptic of your claim." Though he showed foremost reluctance, he did however slow his inhale and exhalations, perhaps by subconscious unknowing or perhaps by conscious resolve derived by the doctor's assertion. And as before, Dr. Sortelli had already disappeared, whether he heard the last words or not was uncertain, but it already seemed that this doctor was a man with esteem for his abilities and would have prepared the tonic with or without disbelief by the patient.

After a few minutes of absence Dr. Sortelli descended the stairs to find the stout, double-chinned elder man clutching his chest, doubled in the chair in severe pain. His breathing once again heavy and labored, he took the jelly-jar sized decanter from the doctor without forewarning and began drinking. His eyes grew wider as the liquid hit his buds and sank down his throat, if the tonic had a coarse taste, he was beyond caring. Thanking the kind doctor, he asked for how he may pay for the serves to which Sortelli replied, "Sir, I ask for nothing other than your good health and that you return so I can witness with my own eyes and for my own mind the properties of the tonic's effects."

The thin and nimble young doctor smirked as he ended his seemingly rehearsed sentence, his thick mustache cocked to the side as his lips tightened in an awkward slant. He helped Mr. Richmond to his feet and watched as the elder man struggled to carry on to the street, refusing any further kind gestures with a polite thank you and goodbye.

It was obvious to the doctor that his tonic had already begun to set in by the refusal of further assistance.

***

The next morning Dr. Sortelli woke to a knocking upon his door. It was Mr. Richmond with a giant smile and a check for five-hundred dollars. "Doctor, I must confess that when I left I had already begun to feel the positive effects of your tonic and when I found my way to bed I was completely free of pain and slept the night full and deep."

The elder man paced across the dimly lit room, a smile upon his face as he scanned over the contents: a small circular wooden table with two wooden chairs opposite one another, a window —the window from where he was originally beckoned-- with the dark black curtains pulled to the side, similar dark black curtains which looked like thin lace on the other end of the room and a door, which he could only assume led to the additional interior of the apartment.

Dr. Sortelli, still in his nightwear and peppered with sleep, pardoned himself and left through the door to return moments later fully dressed. He held the check in his hand, extended towards his patient. "Mr. Richmond," he read off the check, "I cannot accept this very generous amount."

Mr. Richmond stood silent and a baffled look came about his features as he took the check between his thick, short fingers. "But certainly as a doctor you are inclined to charge for your services?"

"I am."

"And the services you provided to me were more than exceptional. This is not only payment for your services but a gift from an indebted man."

"Sir, I must admit I do not feel comfortable." Dr. Sortelli took an exaggerated step off to the side and raised a hand to his mouth. "If I had been the creator of the tonic, then I would be more inclined to accept your very generous offer."

Taking a step closer to the doctor, the baffled look still apparent on his face, Mr. Richmond asked, "I must understand, doctor. You did not mix this tonic yourself?"

"I did, but I did not come upon this concoction by my own mind and hand."

"I'm sorry... I do not understand."

"You see, Mr. Richmond. I am a doctor of medicines it is true, but I am also..."

"Yes?"

A hint of embarrassment came upon the younger man, "To be honest I had the help of spirits. I am a medium, I was guided by the voices of the dead."

"Spirits?"

Dr. Sortelli glanced at the elder man and then made for the table where he gestured toward the opposite seat. Mr. Richmond obliged, his attention held by curiosity. "You see," the doctor began as he sat, "I am a vessel for the spirits. They communicate with me and I with them." He held his gaze on the other man, awaiting a response. "It was by the spirits' guide that I concocted that exact tonic I gave you last night only hours before our meeting and... I believe that they gave me this tonic specifically for you, as though they knew of our encounter to come."

"What, may I ask, was in the tonic?" said an enthusiastic Mr. Richmond.

"That I do not know myself. It was as if they guided my hands and as though no time had passed and then, the tonic was there waiting for you. I am sorry I cannot provide more information."

Mr. Richmond sat speechless, staring at the tabletop and, Dr. Sortelli staring at the elder man.

It was a few moments before the stout man softly asked, his gaze held on the table, if these spirits ever appeared as physically entities. When it was confirmed they did in fact psychically appear for the doctor when he had summoned them, his eyes turned upward to meet those of the doctor and his mouth formed a crude outline of a smile. "You see, doctor, I ask only because I recently lost my wife. It's been nearly more than a year since her passing and I find myself growing not only old, but lonely as well."

"I'm very sorry for your lose."

Mr. Richmond extended his arm across the table, the check in his hand, "Please, Dr. Sortelli, make her manifest for me. Please, I beg you. For one last farewell between she and I."

Dr. Sortelli stared at the check and then reluctantly accepted it. "I'll need a few days. And, you must understand it is the spirits who choose to appear I cannot promise that you will see your deceased wife, I am merely a vessel for communication."

"I understand," he nodded, the fat of his neck climbing his chin, "I understand."

"What is your wife's name?"

"Evelyn. Evelyn Marie Richmond." His face filled then, with excitement. "Oh, oh doctor you have no idea how pleased you have made me."

As he stood Dr. Sortelli asked that the elder man come back in two days' time and at the strike of twelve o'clock of that night, he shall summon Evelyn and if she chooses to communicate, she may also manifest herself physically for her dear husband to gaze upon.

***

At the *World's Fair: Columbian Exposition*, the very first servings of a popcorn, peanut and molasses mixture that would come to be known as *Cracker Jack* was served to visitors upon the midway and, at *Buffalo Bill's Wild West Show* Annie Oakley split playing cards in half edge-wise with a .22 caliber rifle. All the day's activities and entertainment went unnoticed to Mr. Richmond as he waited less than patiently, his eagerness equal to that of a small child on holiday.

He paced his hotel room, stopping only to check his pocket watch and to sip from the decanter of tonic, a glass jelly-jar once full of watered-down *Dr. Pepper* soda pop and liquid opium tincture.

***

Palms sweating within the strong grasp of the doctor's hands, his eyes held closed, he listened to the doctor summon the spirit of his deceased wife. "Spirits of the otherworld, please hear me beckon for Evelyn Marie Richmond, dear departed wife of Mr. Darrion Richmond. Spirits, please guide me in contact with Mrs. Evelyn Marie Richmond that she may once again be with her husband in undying love." The table shook and the elder man gasped yet held his eyes closed as instructed by Dr. Sortelli beforehand. "Evelyn Marie Richmond, I beckon you to appear for me, for your husband, Darrion. Evelyn... Return! Return to our world. Return to your husband! Return!"

The table ceased to shake and the doctor released Mr. Richmond's hands. When the man opened his eyes he saw the doctor staring off to the side in utter exasperation, staring to the end of the room opposite the window. He turned his head and though he could not see past the illumination of the flame from the single candle upon the table, he knew there was a presence there. He could feel the presence. He could even smell the presence, the scent of a woman. "Evelyn?" he called out into the dark. He stood and took a hesitant step toward the darkness and as his eyes grew accustom he made out a faint outline of a body behind the thin black lace curtains. As his eyes quickly grew evermore adept to the darkness it became evident the presence was that of a female body. "Evelyn, oh, Evelyn!" he cried, reaching out, grabbing for the shape in the outline.

"No!" Dr. Sortelli scowled. "You must not touch the spirits!" He grabbed hold of the elder man's arm and pulled him back, expelling more effort than he had anticipated, the elder man reluctant to retreat from the spirit. "No, you must have permission from the spirits before bodily engagement."

The elder man turned to the doctor, "It's her, it's Evelyn!" He returned his attention back to the spirit, but she was gone. There was no outline of a body behind the black lace though the scent remained in the air. "Evelyn?" Dr. Sortelli held him back from approaching the black lace. "I can smell her, she's still here."

"No, she has gone." He reeled him backwards, "She has gone. Please, Mr. Richmond, please sit down."

The elder man stood there in the middle of the room, his arms at his sides and his enthusiasm distilled. He turned and sat, "It was her, Evelyn." A look of uncertainty was then brought to the doctor. "It was Evelyn, wasn't it?" He spoke the line as more a statement than a question.

"Yes," the doctor agreed from his seat across the table. "It was Evelyn, your departed wife."

"Why, why then did she leave? I do not understand. Please, conjure her back to me, I must see her. I must embrace her," he pleaded.

"I'm sorry, Mr. Richmond. But you must not touch the spirits without permission from the spirits. It was Evelyn, but she was drawn back to her world when you broke the boundaries. I apologize... I should have warned you."

Mr. Richmond in emotional distress made Dr. Sortelli an offer of twice the amount he gave for the tonic. One-thousand dollars to conjure her back to our world, our realm, to allow him to embrace his dearly loved wife once more... To once more hear her voice, to once more feel her skin, to once more kiss her lips. Once more, he boldly stated, to have one last sexual exchange.

One-thousand dollars to conjure his deceased wife back to the realm of the living for intercourse.

Dr. Sortelli agreed and once again gave the same instructions he had given prior. To return in two days' time and at the strike of twelve o'clock of that night, he shall summon Evelyn and if she chooses to communicate, she may also manifest herself physically for her dear husband. And, if the spirits give permission he may get his wish to have one last sexual encounter with the psychical manifestation of his departed wife.

***

On the midway at the *World's Fair: Columbian Exposition*, the first American beef patties were sandwiched between bread and served as what would come to be known as the hamburger and, at *Buffalo Bill's Wild West Show* Sitting Bull rode around the arena atop his horse, all the while cursing the white man in his native language of Lakota. This, of course went unseen by the traveler from Utica, New York. The elderly Mr. Richmond sat on the bed of his hotel room holding the empty decanter of soda pop and opium. His pulse raced with impatience and excitement of the night's proceedings.

In the front parlor room, Robert Southstead greased the sprockets below the circular table as he briefed his wife and partner on the séance and manifestation. She had hesitantly agreed to the elder man's wishes once the amount of money was honestly acknowledged, one-thousand dollars. Five hundred dollars to Robert for his role in reeling in the elder man and summoning the spirits and five hundred dollars to her for her role as Evelyn, agreeing to allow Mr. Richmond to have intercourse with her behind the black lace curtains where her features could not possibly be seen other than an outline.

Though she disliked the ideal of playing an artificial spirit manifested for an encounter with an elderly man, her liking of money saw past the absurdity.

***

Dr. Sortelli grasped the elder man's hands and told him to close his eyes and mentally beckon Evelyn, to visualize her in his mind as he beckoned her to manifest herself physically in the world of the living.

The candle danced and twirled, sparks jumped and popped, bringing a dim illumination upon the near surroundings.

He began to chant, "Spirits of the otherworld, please hear me beckon for Evelyn Marie Richmond, dear departed wife of Mr. Darrion Richmond. Spirits, please guide me in contact with Mrs. Evelyn Marie Richmond that she may once again be with her husband in undying love." As planned, the table shook and this time there was no gasp from the elder man and his eyes remained tightly shut. "Evelyn Marie Richmond, I beckon you to appear for me, for your husband, Darrion. Appear and embrace your husband. Return, Evelyn! Return to our world. Return and allow your grieving husband one last caress with you, you who he so loves to this very night. Evelyn... Return!"

As before, the table ceased to shake and Dr. Sortelli released the clammy palms of the elder man and this time, when Mr. Richmond opened his eyes, his head was already facing the side of the room with the lace curtains. In expectation, as though he had no doubts that she would appear, no doubts of the doctor's ability to conjure the dead and knew she would physically manifest in the world of the living and allow him one last encounter with her in the most intimate of ways.

He stood silent and approached the darkness. He stopped a few feet from the table and gave his pupils time to adapt before reaching out for the outline of the female body concealed behind the lace. "Evelyn, it's you," he said, perhaps to her or, perhaps to himself. He sniffed the air, "I can smell you." He brushed a hand down the side of the spirit's body, along the outline coated by lace. "I can feel you." The elder man turned his head ever so slightly, "Dr. Sortelli?"

"Yes?"

"Would you please be as kind to give my wife and I time together... Alone."

Dr. Sortelli stood and began through the door to the inner apartment when he was called after once again. "Dr. Sortelli. Thank you." The doctor did not respond, but continued through the door and gently closed it and leaned against the wall with a smile and expelled a soft laugh.

Suddenly, there came a scream from the front parlor and before he could process the sound, the door flung open and the nude spirit manifestation of Evelyn Marie Richmond sprinted into the room and stood before Dr. Sortelli. Tears streaked her face, she held her arms across her breasts, subconsciously fretful of who may see her exposed skin. "Robert!" She yelled, "Robert, I think he's dead!"

He pushed himself from the wall, "What?"

"I felt was his body push up against me and then he moaned and fell to the floor. Oh my god, oh my god I think he's dead."

Robert entered the parlor room and in the dim light could make out the body of Mr. Richmond on the floor, motionless, a hand clenching his shirt above his heart in a death-grip. He knelt beside him and pressed his index and middle fingers against the elder man's neck, against the carotid artery. There was no pulse. "Mr. Richmond?" There was no answer. "Oh no... Mr. Richmond?"

Robert's wife, now clothed, softly approached. "Is he... Is he dead?"

Robert Southstead nodded. "I'm afraid he is. Appears his heart gave out." He stood and gave the body a once over then looked to his wife, "Help me, we have to get him out of here."

He descended first, backwards down the stairs, the elder man's body slumped in his arms, legs suspended by his wife, hooked under her inner elbows. Before they exited the building, he took a quick look up and down the street and when Robert felt it was safe to assume there were no witnesses, they placed Mr. Richmond's body on the sidewalk, his hand still clenching the shirt above his heart.

A passerby in the morning would come along and gather a crowd and summon the police, who would rule out any foul play and not bother with an investigation in the death of a well-dressed vagabond who evidently died of heart failure. This, Robert assured his wife, is how this situation would play out before returning upstairs for a sleepless night.

***

It was 1893 and the city of Chicago was center stage as the *World's Fair: Columbian Exposition* drew millions of visitors from around the globe to wander the streets of *The White City*. On the midway, humorist and poet Benjamin Franklin King, Jr. amused viewers and, at *Buffalo Bill's Wild West Show* Buffalo Bill himself lead a posse of courageous cowboys against an Indian attack. On the south side, Robert Southstead was investigated by the police concerning the death of prominent railroad magnate, Mr. Darrion Richmond and, upon lack of evidence was released on the condition that he and his wife take their show and leave town immediately never to return.

Ten years later the mysterious illusionist and magician Chang Foo Chen was killed onstage at an opera house during a routine bullet-catching trick. The bullet had been fired from a rigged gun, shot by his American wife and partner. His last words, spoken in English, confused the European crowd and sent rumors circulating around the globe as to who had really died that night on the stage. Was it the enigmatic oriental, Chang Foo Chen? The long-lost Dr. Sortelli? Or could it possibly have been the banished Robert Southstead? The rumors still circulate today along with his infamous and curious last words, "It is you? Darrion... Richmond..."

Rerun

Slouched in a recliner, my legs stretched out and feet resting on the floor, I flick through the channels to settle on the channel from where I originally began my search. Discontent yet conceded, I relax and begin to calm my brain for a nap, but as my eyes adjust, I notice a small drip from the television screen, then another, and then another. The speed of the drips quickens and turns into a flow of thick liquid. The rerun in the screen has become nothing more than black and white that submerges my feet and solidifies like wax as fresh liquid pours atop. In vain I attempt to free myself as it rises to my knees, to my waist, to my chest and finally submerges me entirely. I'm immobile as the last of the liquid hardens and from my final gasp a bubble expands, drifts slightly upward before ceasing and, as my consciousness begins to fade I recognize that this is no freak mishap.

This is a gift for and from me to the modern world. I've become encased in this wax for all to see, for generation after generation to observe in equal parts gratitude and empathy... like a television rerun.

AWAKE AND DREAMING

Am I awake? Or am I dreaming I'm awake? Am I awake with the book resting on the bed beside me and the flashlight shining, illuminating the poster on the wall... or asleep and dreaming that I'm awake with the book resting on the bed beside me and the flashlight shining, illuminating the poster on the wall... or am I awake and dreaming of being asleep and dreaming that I'm awake with the book resting on the bed beside me and the flashlight shining, illuminating the poster on the wall?

SLEEPER'S COMPASS

The rain felt refreshing on that humid August night. Again I had found myself walking along the cracked sidewalks of the city. The houses quiet and dark, and in this particular neighborhood they sat entirely too close to one another, allowing only enough space for a small paved walkway to the backs of the houses; the paint chipped or nonexistent in their dilapidated states, sofas and torn recliners resting on the warped porches. This wasn't my side of town, but in a way it felt as if it was. I lived uptown, in a definitive middle class quarter with freshly cut grass and decorative mailboxes. There was nothing special about my residence and its neighbors, the plain and simple lifestyle expressed by our exterior décors, our Americana only stood to fall in play with what was expected. To mow the lawn a day earlier than the surrounding lawns, to expose more flair with ornaments and dangle enough holiday lights to keep from looking out of place.

But here, in this neighborhood I found honesty. What took place inside these homes was shown on the outside and not hidden in a fake smile behind whitened teeth. It was gritty and perhaps that was the reason my walks followed this route on nights I couldn't sleep, which had become every night. Maybe I wanted to, or needed to see what it was like to live outside of a painting.

Insomnia comes to us all every now and then and usually restricts its visits. Though in my case this visitor had moved in and made itself at home. Of course, the medications gave me a night or two of on and off rest, but it never lasted. I flip-flopped from one sleeping aid to another, slight relief came though eventually disappeared as tolerance built up. Soon there were none left and out of pure despair I began taking up constructive hobbies in attempt to save my sanity. I took long drives in the mountains surrounding the city, sometimes driving through the empty downtown streets of nearby towns hoping sleep would come and force me off the road. Puzzles were pieced together and models were built, books were read and horrible rhyming poetry was written. Video games became frustrating and television a complete drain of self-esteem once the infomercials started. By no means an artist, more than a few sketches were crumpled up or torn and tossed in the trash... but circles, the redundant scrawling of overlapping circles, though not providing sleep, gave some relief to my chattering brain. Beside my bed are several composition books filled with nothing but that same spiral pattern, page after page after page.

Once the hallucinations started, I decided that taking drives through the mountainside weren't such a good idea and began going for walks; every night a step further out of my neighborhood. As I wandered down roads I found the redundancy that haunted my insomnia was also present in solid form under the full moon and streetlights, revealing the supreme insecurities of these homeowners. To rid myself of this bourdon I became a bit adventures and strayed into backyards. Sneaking past motion lights and crawling quietly over fences. If there was a playset the swings were put to use, moaning under my weight and groaning as I swayed back and forth. In others, I'd rearrange plastic chairs and when I would find neighboring homes with similar sets, I'd move one to the other to cause confusion and in one particular case, arranged a set of chairs and table from one home on the back deck of another, looking to stir up some harmless trouble. I never stayed too long in one place in worry of being caught.

There was no obvious form of border from one neighborhood to another, only the gradual regression of the environment and atmosphere followed by the decline of the homes themselves. The first night out of my own neighborhood had been discovered as I stumbled over an uneven slab of sidewalk, which had a growth of grass and weeds in cracks and margins. Until this stumble, I hadn't been aware of the change in surroundings. When I slowed my pace and took a look around, it then occurred to me how far I had wandered.

It was in this neighborhood that I came upon the building, awkwardly placed between two blocks of houses on its own lot, a concrete and dirt island. Clearly abandoned, its windows were broken and the grey concrete was chipped and worn, graffiti brought the only color along the first level. Mostly crude toys and throw-ups by writers crafting their skills on the gallery, though there were a few gang tags there were also some nice pieces by experienced artists to fill the balance. A razor-wire fence surrounded it, though several large holes had been snipped and the thick rusted chains that held the gate together had been cut, leaving the gate half open. It seemed to me that whatever this building had been, it was of no concern to the city and had not been for several years, possibly decades. My natural curiosity brought me to the windows, walking from one to another attempting to get the best view I could. When I rounded the building I found an entrance where a door once stood, now an empty passage into an ever-growing darkness. I was curious and bold in my sleepless adventures thus far, yet I could not find the courage to enter the abyss.

When I turned away to continue on with my walk, an illumination from behind threw my shadow on the ground. Jolted, I whirled around. There was no light, no bulbs were lit, no flashlights were pointed, not even a fire burned but somehow there inside the building an eerie pale-blue illumination that I can only describe as that of what I imagine swamp gas may appear rendered the interior of the building visible. With this sudden strange occurrence, my courage was not heightened, but tossed aside by an irresistible captivation. Neglecting common sense, I wandered inside with awe.

The interior, once smooth concrete was now worn and fragment. Surprisingly, though worn, the ceiling held itself well while the floor was slick in places and littered with garbage: cigarette butts, condoms, shattered glass bottles lighters, needles and spray cans just a few of the more unpleasant objects. There were even items of clothing and other material left by squatters such as sleeping bags and pizza boxes, newspapers and beer cans. Bits and pieces of life, remnants of the lives that had somehow found their way here and apparently abandoned the building as the original owners had. As I walked, I let my fingers slide across the wall, caressing the decay.

I went from room to room, hoping to discover hidden secrets. There were none of course, only more random items and the occasional piece of graffiti. And though I knew not what I looked for nor hoped to find, with each knew room I felt my pulse race, felt it peak as I entered and felt it slow as I found nothing. This beat repeated room after room until I had gone to the end of the hallway where a staircase once stood, several feet above my head the stairs ended, crumbling as if made of sand and, giving off the illusion of floating. Perplexed, I stood and stared, the ruins of the last flight at my feet and the concrete trickling to the floor like sand in an hourglass. What I found most troubling was though the staircase was decomposing before my very eyes, it did not change or decrease, the sand never-ending like water down a mountain stream.

As I watched in bewilderment, my eyes fell prey to the monotonous movement and I began to drift off. Still standing, I experienced the wonderful feeling of sleep overcome my body. I was relaxed, my breathing became lighter, slower, a tingling sensation hit my skin and my eyes closed. Before I knew it, the feeling of falling had come and my eyes opened when I stumbled to the ground. The falling sensation was in fact due to falling. First I wondered where I was before regaining my sense and second, I wondered how long I had been asleep on my feet. Luckily the impact of the fall was not great and I was unharmed. When I stood back up, the staircase was still flowing and though I was just as bewildered, I began walking back towards where I had entered.

Perhaps it was due to the sleep deprivation, or perhaps the mystery of the staircase and even the mundane, featureless rooms can't be counted out, but it wasn't until I began back down the hallway from which I came that it occurred to me that I hadn't yet found any possible explanation for the strange pale-blue illumination. I hadn't yet thought more on the subject, taken aback by the odyssey I passed through on the only accessible level, giving it no more attention than I had at first glimpse. Now that I had brought about finding a source of this oddity, had I realized as well, that there were no crossing, merging or adjacent hallways, only the one long, straight passage. It also became noticeable that exhaustion was setting in. I was squinting, my eyes stung and a tightness wrapped around my head, the pain fully registering now that the initial excitement had begun to dwindle.

As I began to recheck the rooms, I found nothing to have changed. Though I had an assumption that whatever it was that I was searching for would not be found, I continued to scan the rooms. When the entranceway came within sight I began to accept that the mysteries I was searching to explain were not obtainable. And when I passed the last, or if be the other way around, the first room, I didn't even bother to step inside, a passing glance sufficient to my tired mind and beaten spirit.

Just as I was about to cross the verge into the outside world, there came an abrupt noise, a ravenous cackle. My eyes popped open wide for a brief moment, and for that brief moment the sting in my eyes and the throb in my head intensified tenfold. Turning toward the noise I blinked and when the purple-blackness of the back of my eyelids lifted, I had come to be in the first room.

An old man sat in the corner atop crumpled pizza boxes, he had a long unkempt beard with crumbs scattered throughout, his skin was pale and wrinkled, the bags under his eyes drooped and his sclerae were completely bloodshot. His hair, white as his beard, fell just short of his shoulders. He was thin, frail, not short but no taller than I. He wore a grey sweatshirt that had several stains that appeared to be dark and wet, his jeans faded and frayed at the bottoms and, he wore only one shoe with a large hole in the palm of the sole. The other shoe he held in his hand. It was then, at the sight of his shoeless, sockless foot that an eerie feeling crept over me. A scar, rough and off-color ran the length and when he noticed that I had seen the scar, he laughed again and lifted his leg, sticking his scarred foot towards me and smacking the shoe against it, as to make sure I was completely aware of the old wound. A devious grin formed on his face and he laughed more loudly.

For a fraction of a heartbeat, I thought back to one summer night when I was 16-years-old. I had snuck out of the house to go to a party at the beach. There were many of us, too many. Rebellious high school kids drinking and getting high, thinking all was well and we were more than cool. And when the police showed up, a pair of Environmental Conservation Officers, the crowd fled, tossing their longneck bottles and dropping their joints in the sand. As I tried to cross the beach, I stepped on a broken beer bottle and it thrust itself deep into my foot. I was spared any legal action due to my age and, pain broadened by embarrassment was to be my punishment.

We stared at one another for a moment, he laughing and I silent. In disbelief, I pulled my hands out in front of me, looked down, down at my grey sweatshirt, at my jeans and my shoes, I rubbed my scarred foot with the toe of the other and felt a phantom itch. He stood and began limping towards me, the grin on his wrinkled face growing with each one-shoed step. He reached out towards me, laughing.

That's when I spun and ran. I ran as far as fear would bring me, out onto the dirt and concrete lot, around the corner to the front of the building, through the snipped fence and down the cracked sidewalk. When I reached the end of the block I doubled over, out of breath, my exhaustion kept temporally at bay by the fear induced rush. The whole while expecting the old man to come chasing, one shoe on the other shoe off, held at the ready to beat me into a stupor, to knock me down and to stuff that scarred foot in my face and then suddenly, it all consumed me. The exhaustion of days and nights spent sleepless, the forlorn hobbies, the endless walking and backyard adventures, the curious and bewildering and unexplainable findings and mysteries of the building, the headache and the heavy eyes... At once they all consumed me and I was out.

I awoke to the sensation of falling and indeed I had fallen. I sat on the floor, rubbing my eyes, the staircase hovering above me, the concrete flowing like sand in an hourglass and I wondered how long I had been asleep.

I did not have to wonder upon where I was.

SLEEPING

Sleeping, I see myself gray as a ghost, stranded on the outskirts of this perverse community in which I reside. Wondering where I have been for so long and why I have felt so ill for reasons I can't understand, nor will, nor would want to understand and, whether or not to awaken and allow myself to communicate these unconscious ambitions or continue to sleepwalk; stranded, gray as a ghost watching my dreams pass by.

FOUND AND LOST

I found angel wings in the bed sheets... Lost, as lost as their names, as lost as the color of their eyes, as lost as the smell of their hair...

I found angel wings in the bed sheets, but they did not fit when I tried them on.

COLON/PARENTHESES (A LOVE STORY)

The tank is almost empty, a tire is leaking air ··a knocking/thumping from the rear·· and there is an hour and a half to go with cruise control on 72mph. Outside, a wintry mix falls from 2 A.M. darkness, dreary and cold. Inside, it is comfortable. Time passes easily when you're happy. Worries fade away like gas fumes into the night air. Indecision moves my hand from steering wheel to radio, incapable to capture the mood(s) I'm in properly through music, I retreat to the sound of the wheels spinning, rolling furiously across the wet pavement. Oddly, the hum is soothing. My mind drifts as I enter the highway via the thruway, drifts off as the knocking/thumping from the rear is covered by the soothing hum...

...The store is not where I want to be after a three-hour drive, though, when I'm with her, with Ashley, the lovely brunette with brown eyes it's not a thought. When I'm with her, I'm with her and that's all and nothing else matters. I'm in her presence and I'm with her, there is no store, no customers or employees, no walls or shelves or ceilings, it's she and I and that is how it is when I'm with her... it's her, I'm with her and only her. She makes it special...

...I hear her gloom and it saddens me. What I can give is material, flowers, artwork and whatever else will come. Though what I can provide is pure: an ear, a voice, a kiss, a hug... a smile. It has not been long, but she has me. Maybe too fast, maybe not, maybe this is what we both need. I

believe it is and I hope she feels it, too. If not now, then someday...

...We caress under blankets, warmth from our bare bodies keeps the cold air at bay. I want her. To pleasure her, to be pleasured by her. She is beautiful and her body seduces me, her curves enhance me like... Oxytocin rising into animalistic adrenaline, pumping through my veins. Hours will pass and when it's over, the blankets are on the floor and I want more of her, though physically I'm unable to do so, covered in a film of sweat and dehydrated. My legs shake beneath my weight. She is divine, I can't feel or eye enough of her and as I vocalize my gestures, she brushes them off and I do not know if it's modesty or not and truly I hope she realizes how wonderful she is and how happy I am to be here with her sharing this time together...

...Exhaustion escalates and sleep comes quickly and she closes her eyes. I know she tried to stay awake for me but she gives to the world so much without asking and I -- selfishly?--worry about keeping her awake on only a few hours' sleep from nights previous. I want to snuggle, to cuddle, to feel our bodies melt together like candle wax. I can't reach her and to do so would awaken her, I curl up and hope her arm falls across my chest, hope her breath finds the back of my neck...

...Playful, smiling, flirting, never would I have thought such joy could be alive within a dull and plain building as this. She brought it to life when she entered, I behind her, following -- always following. She brought color into this world of ashen sterilization and gave it beauty and life. I admire that...

...Her laugh caught me off guard, I've heard her laugh but to hear it loud and genuine and true made me smile and laugh softly to myself, feeling good that I had a part in it...

...There is no "our place" for as long as I'm with her, any place is "our place." She makes it special. She makes it ours...

...She is beautiful and fun, she is clever and sexy, she is artistic and creative, she is caring and giving, she inspires and aspires. She is ·· mine? She is individual... She is...

...She is...

...Indecisive and withdrawn, confused behavior unlike herself. She describes walls, mental walls which are unbreakable, constructed after a previous relationship and though they want to fall, remain strong. Our progression must slow to a reasonable speed. I must accept this and we must disassociate ourselves from what we have...

The car runs on fumes the last few miles and I roll up the driveway, deciding I will wait until the next day to fill the leaking tire. I grab my bags from the back seat, finger the key into the lock, and wonder when I will see her next or, more likely when she will allow me in her presence as a lover lost in life.

Until then, I'll turn off her phone and slip it into her Marc Jacobs clutch and place the handheld transceiver beside my bed. For when she retires her withdrawn indecisiveness, tears down those walls to disassociate ··then reassess·· and resuscitate our relationship.

That, or I wonder... the winter's cold ··felt from inside the trunk of my car·· becomes too bitter for a single thermal blanket.

A MIDNIGHT DRIVE

A midnight drive to sooth a rambling mind and air a constricted heart. South, to Albany; south past 1E I'm not slowing. New York City, wide awake I drive on. Surprisingly the New Jersey Turnpike isn't cramped at 6a.m. and I find that the sun rising over storage units in Delaware is appeasing and scenic. Crossing into Maryland, I yawn —' Baltimore, 65 miles. Drifting off 55B I spot a motel and find a room. I lie in bed at 10a.m. and pop 20mgs of Ambien and 100mgs of Seroquil and stare at the ceiling for two hours. I wake moments after my eyes close, limbs and mind are dead. Alone, sick, scared and depressed... I'm tired, so very, very tired and alone in Bodymore, Murderland.

SOMETIMES

Sometimes when you're driving alone it's hard not to drift off. With the radio silent and the night air crisp and quiet, your eyes easily fall prey to the monotony of the lane divide lines. Then soon enough, without comprehension, your mind succumbs to their hypnotic repetitions. Usually you drift for several minutes without ever knowing it. Other times you're snapped back into reality confused and frightened, a cacophony of metal scrapping against metal, the shattering of the windshield and streaks of blood across the hood of your car.

IN STRIDES

He came unannounced.

Long strides down the pavement his worn black sneakers kicking up sand collected and swept to the side of the street from the previous winter by months of passing cars.

He wore a smile, not small yet not large. A genuine smile, happy, content. His khaki cargo pants dotted with holes, flapped with each step showing the outline of his slender, muscular legs. A thin black t-shirt under a red and white flannel, unbuttoned. The sleeves rolled up his tanned, tattooed forearms. Blue-gray artwork obscured as only half seen. Tight to his back a gray backpack, many pockets and zippers surely stored provisions and the necessities of materialism. Shoulder-length dark hair, a widow's peak draping bangs to the sides with brown eyes to match.

Mrs. Longbow --a young wife and mother who revealed too much skin for a wife and mother-- two houses down trimming her roses at the edge of her lawn stood from her knees, stood at the fence and watched. The shears dropping to the ground as he caught her motion and spared a wave from a distance. She stepped backwards, feet cautious and then sprung. Twirled around and made for the front door. Leaving the shears in the soil. The door slammed shut and the curtains spread open and she watched from the window.

He passed the first house, the Winston place, and continued on. His stride not missing a beat.

A lawnmower engine started a few houses up around the bend and I dared not look, leave my perch to see where it came from exactly. I noticed a curtain across the street flap quick enough for a scan to spot the noise. Mr. Johnston, a man who I shared several uncomfortable open-air chance moments with over the years of my residence on Blossom Blvd. A tubby, short man of elder years with an appetite for late night movies that shone through the glass and onto the dark street in faint projections.

As he approached the second house, heels kicking up sand to float among moats of dust and pollen, smile shimmering in the morning light of a warm, sunny summer day, he glanced to the windows. Head tilting, neck craning then turning from the home of the late widow Cranston to look across the street at the parallel home of Mr. and Mrs. Wright. A white split-level with blue trim and the greenest of lawns perfectly trimmed and shrubs groomed almost too pristine. (The inspiration and driving jealousy of the lawnmower around the bend, playing catch up with the neighborhood. Hoping the wandering eyes between blinds had not yet befallen its unkemptness.)

Again, the stranger waved and to whom I only assume one or more likely both of the Wrights as they watched from within the protection of their home, keypad and phone both at the ready.

Growing closer he lolled his head back and closed his eyes, allowing his face full exposure to the glory of the rays from above. He basked in that moment, his smile opening to show teeth, gum, tongue and darkness until he walked into the hedges of Mrs. Hayes. He jerked to a halt and laughed.

Ran the palms of his hands over the top of the even cut hedge, fingers dipping down inside their crevices and plucked a leaf.

He *plucked* a *leaf.*

Plucked a *leaf.*

Rolled it between his fingers, let it drop and continued walking. Quickening each step to match his previous passing stride, his hand brushing across the top of the shrub. At the end of the hedge he let his hand stay in the air, gliding up and down every few paces as if running along the top of invisible shrubbery... grazing

He *plucked* a *leaf.*

Set in his pace he strode on. Examining the bushes, trees and the lawns. The driveways, walkways, fences and the homes themselves: white split-levels with blue trim built into the slight hill our neighborhood was founded upon during Eisenhower's presidential terms. (The golden years when confidence and compliance dictated the outcome of position and prominence.)

The stranger seemed to have a glow about him. A child in wonderment of the awe-inspiring intrigue that is a carnival midway. The sights and sounds and smells stimulating every sense to its limit. A rush, almost overwhelming in bliss. The stranger glowed in this child-like aura. His eyes wide, his lips curled and his body language frantic with energy yet held within, constrained for what I hesitated to assume, self-decency.

As he came upon the white picket fence of the transplanted southern couple, the Bartlett's, an abrupt barking of dogs jolted him. He flinched and stumbled sideways towards the center of the road and stopped to stare in an odd, confident manner at the two large Rottweilers as they jumped, pawed at the fence and barked. He watched them protecting them and theirs, their property and their masters without movement.

Staring. Not frightened, but curious.

Staring...

The front door opened and Mr. Bartlett appeared to assess the situation, but upon sight of the stranger, ceased his words and slammed the door and watched through the front window as the stranger did the most unthinkable.

Slowly, he stepped to the fence and squatted no less than half a foot from it. Though I could not hear him, I could see his lips form an oval and surely cooing the animals in a gentle hush, he extended his hand through the fence. The dogs, one after the other settling, their barks calming, turning from vicious warnings to friendly, playful huffs... hovered together to lick his hand.

They wiggled and wagged their docked tails, huffs turned to whines of attention and after he brought his free hand to his mouth, a finger to his lips to bring them to silence with a gentle shush, they sat. Side by side the beasts sat, motionless and silent as he petted them, one by one as they waited patiently for their noses to be stroked and their ears to be scratched and their heads to be rubbed and as he stood and walked on, they rolled to their backs and pawed at the air, whining for one last caress.

That is when I realized the sputter of the lawnmower had died only seconds before the stranger's encounter with the dogs. I leapt from my vantage point of the living room window and ran to the other side of the room where I drew up the shade to see three houses up, on his lawn, the tall and thick Mr. Murphy. He stood hands to his sides, the lawnmower at arm's length in front of him as he watched the stranger. Who was close enough now on the bend of the road to appear on the horizon. Mr. Murphy turned on his heels and made for his home, keeping his eyes on the stranger through his peripherals.

I ran back to my original post and found that the stranger had stopped. He himself watched as something approached from behind. A brown and white station wagon crept up the road. Mrs. Miller, a tiny, frail widow who had grown old with the home she inhabited since its conception. She spared him no mind as she passed and pulled into her driveway next door to Mr. Johnston, separated by a rustic yet attractive split-rail wooden fence.

The stranger hurried his approach and caught the old woman's car door, he held it open and extended an arm. Mrs. Miller sat there, her heart surely skipping a beat, as surely as her face ··which I could not see·· was an expression of terror. A wrinkled hand, veins thick and blue jutting through emaciated skin, took hold of the stranger's and he slipped his strong arm, snaked it through her own for a solid frame for her to stand. She rose from her seat and with the stranger's guidance, slowly, sure-footedly, made it up the walkway, up the steps, unlocked and opened the front door and together, they disappeared inside.

Together... Inside!

She *allowed* him *inside!*

Inside.

A few moments passed and my heart sank within me until he sprang down the steps and to the car. He closed the driver's door and moved to the tailgate, which he opened and laid flat. Two at a time, one in each arm hugged to his chest the stranger brought Mrs. Miller's groceries ·-double-bagged in brown paper bags·· past the threshold of her home and inside, presumably to her kitchen and then back out, repeating the effort until the very last bag. When he closed the tailgate and again disappeared into the widow's home, she closing the door behind him I looked to the street to see that like I, the neighborhood was not only perplexed but suspicious.

A minute passed. And then another before the shade and curtain of Mrs. Miller's sole bay·style living room window facing my home was opened and light shone in. Allowing me the advantage of peering inside. From the window she took small steps and sat into her recliner. Across from her on the sofa, the stranger. His backpack on the floor resting against a leg of the coffee table between them. On the table was a platter of crackers, cheeses and meats that they shared as they exchanged words and pleasant expressions. The stranger himself held a plate in his lap with the crusts of a sandwich and half·empty glass of milk in his hand.

After a few more minutes of conversation, he placed the plate on the table, on the knitted coffee tablecloth and gathered his pack. She escorted him to the front door where she waited for him to gain his stride on the roadside before waving and closing the door.

I moved to the window of the front door, to watch him as he passed my home and then to the far side of the living room to watch him as he strode further up the hill, his back to me until he came to a sudden stop.

His hands went into the air and his head bobbed as it spoke unheard words. A foot moved backward, the other followed and Mr. Murphy followed in a forward momentum with a pump-action in his hands.

He walked toward the stranger until he crested his lawn, stood beside the lawnmower and watched as the young man, the stranger, the interruption of the normalcy of everyday life on this secluded, reclusive boulevard took cautious steps backward until he turned and broke into a brisk jog down the road, around the bend from where he had come. Mr. Murphy followed to the edge of his lawn in a subtle saunter with the shotgun trained on the stranger until he was out of range.

I hurried to the other window to watch as the stranger slowed his jog to his casual stride, peering over his shoulder while passing the home he had previously been invited into and rewarded, passing the wiggling of excited and playful puffing dogs who whined when he passed without notice and off into the distance from whence he came...

Worn black sneakers kicking up dust behind him as he faded.

IS THIS DEATH?

When I was a small child my family moved out of the city and into a farmhouse in the countryside. Many days were spent discovering the creatures in the wooded acres surrounding my new home and when it was raining or snowing, I searched for secrets in the dusty attic and dank basement.

It was on one of those interior expeditions that I found the door. Inspecting intricate webbing, I found and followed the spider that scrambled along its trap to seek security behind the washing machine. It took all the strength in my frail body, but I managed to spread enough room to open the door.

I crawled into that small room on my hands and knees, with no illumination or tool to gauge its dimensions, coerced only by the curiosity of a child's mind. When I reached a wall I attempted to turn back, but I had gotten disoriented. It was a whole day and night before my father's flashlight stung my eyes and freed me from my dungeon, and after all these years I can still remember the one and only thought that repeated itself into disharmony during my time in that darkened space, terrorized by silence. Over and over again, I wondered, *is this death... is this death... is this death... this is death... this is death... this is...*

FOR YOU

Are you there or are you... *here*, inside of me? An original individualized delusion of a tattered mind. Curious, bored and alone you've been in here for so long... perhaps I know you far too well. Of course, if I bleed you no one will care nor notice the desertion. You are only what is left of a shattered mind once coherent. Though I confess, I've never known anyone who has died.

THE WRESTLER GRAVES

Robin Graves coats his face with black and white grease paint to appear as a skeleton, a skull much like a voodoo priest may wear. As he inspects his work in the mirror of the locker room, the reflection of a gray form streaks across the floor. It's a rat. About the size of a large man's fist, the long tail in fray from battle and perhaps disease. Robin corners the rodent and bends down, leaning in on the frightened animal which wriggles its nose and stares at the shirtless man in skin-tight pleather pants and skull paint. Robin smiles and after a few moments, stands, turns and walks away. Allowing the rat to find its way back from whence it came, and leaving an omen of misfortune.

A trail of rose petals leads to Robin, plucking and gently placing each individual petal to the floor of their apartment hallway. The illumination is soft and gives off a hint of sepia. Scented candles fill the air with a natural aroma, romantic yet unassuming.

Inside the ring, Gregory "Gypsy" Johnson, a behemoth of a man, assaults Robin with a rain of rehearsed kicks and punches, chokes and throws. The grunts of their violent ballet echoing off the walls as four observers watch from outside the ropes.

He leads the trail through the hallway and to the bathtub, where bubbles form atop the steaming water that pours down from the faucet. Next to the bathtub he carefully arranges the roses and between the stems he balances a note in an envelope inscribed to his dearly loved wife.

Maryanne Macgregor-Graves, a curvy blonde beauty, wife and manager of Robin watches the run-through with a stone face as brother and trainer, "Skinny" Steven Graves holds his thin arms across his thin frame, elbows protruding sharp bone. Around the corner stands Bobbi-Jo Breault, the petite and bubbly girlfriend of the larger man and, Alexander Kuts, his Ukrainian-born manager. Though they know the outcome beforehand, they show support and root for their perspective wrestlers in a low-key fashion, as to not distract the men from their work.

Maryanne rests in the bubble-bath, hair pinned up in a bun with her back slouched against the wall. The flowers remain on the floor beside her while she reads the card: "For the beat my heart skipped when we first met. Love, Robin."

Bouncing off the ropes, Robin charges at Johnson and the smaller man is lifted off the ground and in one blunt motion, comes down crooked and headfirst. Hands and arms tangled within those of the larger man, the unrehearsed and unmentioned move finds him off guard without any time for reaction, his forehead catching the weight of his mass, neck crunching up and body falling limp to the side. Before a second's pass, Skinny is quickly making way through the ropes to his brother, breaking the eerie silence in the ring as Johnson peers down at his opponent. Close behind him is the Ukrainian and Bobbi-Jo. Maryanne, shocked immobile and silent, covers her mouth though her eyes, they cry out her husband's name.

Robin is relaxed on the couch, staring at the blank television. He's fully dressed in jeans and a loose black hoodie, white socks peeking through between the cuffs and a pair of dark Saucony's. Attention focused on the screen, he is unaware of his wife standing against the frame of the entryway, a plate in her hand. She watches him with a look of compassion and as the moment passes, what understanding she may have of his injury is thrown to the wind once she approaches him. "Cheese and tomato," she says, extending the plate on which a sandwich and a big white oval pill are placed.

"Cheese and tomato, no crust?" he says, straining his glare.

"No crust."

Robin breaks the seemingly hypnotic trance with the television and looks at his wife, smiles and takes the plate from her, lays it on his lap and fingers the pill. His smile turns into a frown as he pushes the pill around the plate before plucking it, like a child with a vegetable. He speaks not a question, but a verbal reflection, "Another..."

"The doctor said it's best to take it with food."

He nods and drops the pill in his mouth, washes it down with a sip from a can of caffeine free diet Pepsi from the end-table. "Cheese and tomato."

Before she can turn away, Maryanne puts on a pleasant face and asks, "All dressed up and nowhere to go, huh?" He doesn't respond, as though she hasn't spoken at all Robin takes a bite from his sandwich and returns his fixation to the blank television. She drops her pleasantness as she walks away, back into the kitchen from where she entered.

Skinny is sitting at the kitchen table, a wrestling entertainment magazine spread open in front of him. She sits down across from her brother-in-law. "He eatin'?"

"With the pills..." Maryanne sighs, "That seems to be the only way I can get him to eat anything."

"At least it's something," he nods to himself before carrying on. "It's progress." He flips the page, sparing her a supportive roll of the shoulders and a tweak oh his lips. "Some serious shit, frontal lobe damage like that. You heard the doc, he should be dead or 'plegic. Miraculous."

"You're right, he's lucky... We're lucky."

Skinny balls his hand up and raps a fist against the magazine. "Ya know, it gets me."

"Hmm?"

"What really gets me," his tone turns angry, "What really gets me is that this – now I know it was a freak accident and all, but Rob, he was jus' comin' up, ya know." He points to a specific line in the article he's reading and begins to recite, "'In injury news, Robin Graves took a fall to the head during a training session and remains in questionable care. This just two weeks before his WWE debut against Headhunter Maims.'"

"It almost seems surreal." She slides a hand towards Skinny, leaning in to grab his attention from the magazine article that is burning his temper. "Like, if I wasn't there I wouldn't believe it."

"I know, right. Man, if Mom and Pop hadn't set up them funds for us -"

"Fortunately for us, they did," she interrupts.

"If we didn't have them funds," he shakes his head with an exhale, "I don't even wanna think about it, we'd be out on our asses tryin' to recoup from this."

There is a brief moment of silence, a heartbeat. They stare at one another and are jolted by the buzzing of Maryanne's cell phone on the table.

"Speak of the saviors," she says, picking up the phone.

Skinny pushes out his chair and stands, grabbing his coat. "I gotta be goin' anyhow." He heads for the backdoor, "Take care of my bro, now. An' tell Ma I say 'Hello.'" He waves before walking out the door, Maryanne waves back.

She flips the phone open, "Hello."

Half of the sandwich remains uneaten amongst bread crumbs, the plate on the end-table beside the Pepsi can. Robin is hunched forward, hands resting gently on his knees, his stone gaze on the blank television screen. In the background, from the kitchen, his wife speaks on the phone. "Yeah, yeah I can be there." She pauses. "You too, bye."

She appears in the entryway; a coat sleeve hastily being pulled up her arm. She watches him as she adjusts herself, a hint of perplexity and perhaps worry in her expression. "Robin, honey." He is unmoved by her voice. She steps forward and into his line of sight. "Robin, I gotta run out for a while. It's important. I'll be home later tonight, okay?" She starts off before he can reply, though he attempts no such thing, his gaze never breaking. "Love you," she calls out from the kitchen, opening the back door and leaving.

If Maryanne's presence was seen, heard or known, it was no match for the depth in which the television held Robin's eye.

In the parking lot of the apartment complex, Gregory Johnson places his hand behind the passenger seat headrest, giving his full assertion to the woman entering. She shuts the door behind her as she sits with what could be a slam or an accidental slip of the fingers. "How's he doing?" he asks Maryanne.

"I don't know, I don't think it's working," she says, positioning herself in the seat. "Other than zoning off he seems relatively fine."

From the headrest, he brings his hand to her head and attempts to glide in for a kiss. She pushes him away. "Bullshit," he shows agitation toward the gesture and the situation of which they speak. "You're giving him the full dose aren't you?"

"Three times a day, he doesn't seem to -" She breaks midway and is taken by something in her line of sight.

"What?"

She points ahead and Gregory follows her extended digit to see Robin exiting the building. "Now where the hell could he be off to?"

"I'm not sure..."

There are papers scattered across the office, the desk is overturned, a shattered lamp at its side and a wooden chair is broken into nothing more than kindling. The executive leather office chair is cocked, crooked against the bookcase against the rear wall by the shelf. A trail of tarot cards leads to the bathroom where the fury continues. Alexander Kuts, Gypsy's Ukrainian-born manager is bloodied and battered;

he grasps at the toilet bowl for leverage and holds a hand up in front of his face, pleading for an end to his attack being dealt out by Robin. "I swear to you, I don't know what you're talking about," he cowers. "I'm not a real Gypsy, neither is Gregory. It's all a gimmick man, not real. You know that."

Robin relaxes a fist and points to one of the tarot cards, "Then why do you have those?"

Alexander sniffles, wipes a glob of mucus and blood from his nose onto his torn shirt and sniffles again, sucking back tears and mucus. "It's all an act man, like I said it's not real, it's for show. You know this! All of it. Fuck, man. There's no such thing as a Gypsy curse. Jesus... Even if there was how the fuck would I know. I was raised in Jersey!" He raises a hand to accommodate his end statement before bringing it back to guard his face.

Robin brings an open palm slap down across the man's face, atop and over his defending hand before abruptly turning around and walking away.

"Hey, where you going?" Alexander starts to his feet with the help of the toilet. "I hope you're not going where I think you're going."

Robin passes by a wall-mounted plasma and before he gets two strides past, he stops, faces the screen and stares at the blank television screen. The picture pops up and fizzes and skips for a moment before a woman in a white lab coat and mid-calf length skirt appears, her hair pinned up in a bun. Black, rectangle rimmed glasses don her attractive face. She speaks to him. "I told you, Robin. He's telling the truth. It's the pills, it always has been the pills."

"But, how the pills? You gave them to me."

"They switched them. You're being fooled, lied to. Drugged."

"Why would they... Why would she -"

Alexander slides across the wall, he cowers and eyeballs the television before cutting off Robin. "What the fuck..." he mutters, sliding ever so gently closer to his desk. "Who you talking to?"

Robin continues, "Doc, why would Maryanne do that?" The picture once again fizzes and skips, "Doc?" It pops off with a flash. "Doc?" The screen is blank to Robin; he turns to Alexander.

"Who you talking to, man?" He's cowering evermore now. The quiet stare from the wrestler causes a bead of sweat to trickle down the manager's forehead.

The air is an aroma of sexual fragrances, of secretions and perspiration, of friction, latex and water-based lubricants. Gregory Johnson is covered by an off-white colored sheet, his arms spread out like a cross, the women curled up in his massive hold, resting their heads on his pectoral muscles. His girlfriend, Bobbi-Jo and his mistress, Maryanne lay nude atop their lover, themselves half covered by the sheet. They speak to one another: "I still don't understand why you didn't follow him," Bobbi-Jo says.

"Didn't need to," Maryanne replies. "He's been cooped up there most the time, he probably just went for a walk. Probably wanted some fresh air."

"It couldn't have hurt to know."

"Don't worry your pretty little face. Worries cause wrinkles. Besides, he most likely just went to the mall. He's been doing that once in a while, goes to the Best Buy and just stares at the TVs. He says they speak to him or something."

"Jesus... How much of that stuff are you giving him, that Digiti, Digit -"

"It's called, Digitalis," Maryanne explains. "And a lot of it."

Gregory smiles a sinister smile and chuckles. He reaches for the nightstand on the other side of Bobbi-Jo and lifts his radio alarm clock. "Shit!" He sits up, letting the women slide off his body. "I gotta get goin' I'm gonna be late." He crawls out of bed and begins to get dressed.

The women cuddle up together, Bobbi-Jo embraced by Maryanne, the big spoon. "You sure this is gonna do it? I mean... The money, no questions asked? Skinny isn't dumb he's gonna ask questions or put -"

Maryanne interrupts, "You're giving Skinny too much credit. He's a man just like any other man and just like any other man he lets his dick do the thinking."

This seems to ease the more petite of the two, calms her wandering mind. "Yeah, you're probably right."

"Once Robin is gone, Skinny will come right to me, just like we planned. Now your only worry is to make sure you do your part and you leave Skinny to me."

"You're right. And don't you worry," she brings her head up off the pillow to see if her boyfriend is in earshot before continuing. "Gregory won't be a problem, he'll be easy."

They both break for a moment, a pause for possible reaction from the large wrestler if he heard his name mentioned. Satisfied by the silence, they look at one another and lock lips, releasing only to start a duet of soft moaning as their hands roam.

In the living room of the apartment, Robin has found himself without words. There blocking the television is a man of sorts, a man made out of black and white digital snow and like the television he fizzes and skips. The man points to the pill bottle on the end-table and speaks: "Lex talionis."

Robin is unfamiliar with the words yet understands and picks up the bottle. The man is without mass, yet there is a connection between the two, from one conscious to another, from that of a unidimensional being to that of a living, breathing sentient organism. When he turns back to the man, he, it, like the television, fizzes and with one bright white flash, pops and disappears.

In the darkness Maryanne palms the wall for the light switch to the kitchen, it's late and the moon hidden behind plump clouds shines no light through the window. She's startled when she flicks the switch and jumps when the overhead light comes on. Skinny is seated at the table, a cup of coffee in his hand and a cup across from him, full and steaming. "Holy shit, Skinny," she gasps. "You scared the hell out of me." She walks over towards her brother-in-law and begins to remove her jacket.

He pats the table, "Come, sit. We have something to discuss."

"Is everything all right?" She sits, "What are you doing here in the dark anyway?"

"Please, drink. It'll calm you." He waits for Maryanne to lift her cup and take a sip. "It's about Robin -"

"Is he all right?" She acts worried, frenzied, a performance worthy of a Razzie.

"Yes, it's about Robin, and yes he's all right. But we've got something to discuss."

In the stale, chemical treated metallic confines of the gym's locker room, Gregory is alone, his manager nowhere to be found. His locker is popped open, slightly off kilter. Inside there is an unmarked stainless steel water bottle and a note taped to the wall, scribbled in Kuts' handwriting:

You're late. I couldn't wait any longer, not feeling too well. You're on your own tonight.

-Kuts

PS: Try the bottle, it's a new protein I mixed.

He unscrews the polypropylene cap and takes a hesitant drink. He nods, bringing a not-too-shabby expression to his face and he takes another swallow. As he gets undressed from his casual wear into his outfit, he continues to drink until the bottle is empty and placed back into the locker and closed up.

The effects of the concoction hit him as he exits the locker room and heads for the gym. Unusual gurgling and rumbling sound from his stomach, nausea tickles his esophagus and his head is afloat, dizziness and a lack of balance bring him to a stagger. He hugs the wall, making the last few steps out of the hallway and into the main gym. He raises his head and over the machines and the benches and the weights, he sees what first appears as an apparition. The large man shakes his head and closes his eyes, opens and blinks rapidly before finding that apparition is in fact a man and he pushes off from the wall, stumbles toward the ring, stumbles toward the man in the skull face paint waiting for him.

Like a child crawling from a crib, Gregory "Gypsy" Johnson crawls into the ring, using the ropes and buckles to stand himself upright. His head bobs and his eyes blink slowly and mechanically. "The fuck you do to me?" he says with a mumble.

"Lex talionis," Robin says, "Eye for an eye."

"Fuck you."

"You don't look too good. You feelin' okay?"

With a sudden surge of endorphin Gypsy fights the effects, charges Robin Graves and spends a large, lethargic right hook. His opponent easily slips to the side, letting the large man swing at the air and over-stride. "I'll take that as a 'No,'" he teases. Righting himself, the wrestler charges in again with another large, empty swing which the smaller, more agile wrestler catches and then twists, tripping his nemesis in the process, sending him down to the canvas with a loud thump. "If you're feeling this bad, imagine how bad your mistress feels right now." Robin takes a few steps backwards to allow Gypsy to lift himself up using the ropes.

Back in the apartment kitchen, Maryanne is face down on the table. One hand laid outstretched and the other dangling towards the floor. She tries to talk, but only a wet noise escapes her mouth. Skinny is rummaging through her coat pockets and when he finds her cell phone he flips it open and dials 911, placing it next to her as he flicks off the light and walks out. Leaving his sister-in-law paralyzed and dying with only spit bubbles and a slight wet moan to communicate her trouble to the dispatcher who has answered: "911 what is your emergency?" the voice on the other end of the line says. "911, please state your emergency." The dispatcher recognizes the silence and asks that the caller remain on the line until a trace of the phone number can be matched to a place of residence and an officer arrives. The effort is too late, as Maryanne exerts her last breath and closes her eyes for the final time while the unanimous voice continues on.

Johnson stands leaning against the ropes, his weight almost entirely held up by the cable and rubber hosing, his arms dead at his sides. "Now don't be worrying about that girlfriend of yours, Alexander is taking care of that end for me. Turns out he's not such a bad guy. Hell of a manager, I can see what you saw in him. He's handling my comeback. You got me though, you got me good. I loved that woman with all my heart. It took a lot for me to do this, believe me. And I don't mean to you or your little lady, I mean to her, Maryanne."

On that note, Robin bursts into a sprint and leaps into the air, planting a flying, double-legged dropkick on the larger man's chest and knocking him backwards, flipping over the ropes and tumbling down to the cold floor. His head lands first, his neck crunching under the weight of his body.

Robin, the smaller, more agile wrestler slowly gets to his feet and climbs up the turnbuckles to the top and peers down at his target that lies limp and unmoving.

The pretty, petite, Bobbi-Jo answers the rapping upon her door, both opening and answering at once. "Yes?" she says, taking in Alexander's physically askew appearance.

"Hello, Bobbi-Jo." Her eyes squint in curiosity and she moves aside as he proceeds to step forward. "May I come in?" he says, pushing past her and walking into the living room. She shuts the door and follows him, taking notice of the cups of coffee in his hands.

Realization, a Reflection

There is no birth, no yesterday nor past. There is no death, no tomorrow nor future. There is only this present moment of realization... That what is done is done and what will come has come and we are nothing more than that somber mirrored reflection that has embraced the features we learned to loath.

FAITH, DISILLUSION, AND CONTROL (AN INTROSPECTION)

Humankind has made itself overly susceptible to disillusion and accepts unquestioned suggestion and demand should it be from a source of fiction or fact or fancy. From religion or authority, parent or priest, officer or teacher or lover... obedience is a failure by the individual and an obstruction of character. Those who challenge this are outcasts, recluses, loners or simply crazy in the eyes of others, of those who are fully afflicted and consumed by this disillusion and criminals to those who demand and suggest these memes, rules and regulations. Any who partake in differentiating themselves from the herd are unknowingly showing us the way but those who preach about knowing how to go about doing such are bringing conformity just as those who watch over us. There are no set guidelines to freeing oneself, it's not something one can read about or learn by doing, no textbooks or seminars. It's an inborn trait... installed within us upon birth.

A Comic Book

She pulls the blanket up and tucks it tight around his ten-year-old body, kisses him on the forehead and flicks off the light before closing the door behind her. He listens to her footfalls fade, until the very last step ··exactly thirteen·· is taken and shrugs, wiggles and loosens himself free from under the blanket. Running his hand along the edge of the bedside stand he feels the steel loop of the drawer and opens it, feels inside for the flashlight ··he dares not to chance the use of the lamp·· and presses the button. The beam illuminates the drawer and its contents and he pulls out something thin and shiny that was hidden under an illustrated edition of Mark Twain's *The Adventures of Huckleberry Finn*.

Under the sheet and blanket ··hidden from the world, his family and most importantly, his mother·· he peels back a single strip of Scotch tape and is careful not to let it stick to the comic book as he slides it out of its Mylar bag.

In the secrecy and comfort of his fabric cave, he stares at the cover with a sense of awe expressed on his face: eyes large and shimmering, mouth agape and his mind in an equal state of marvel.

He lays it flat on the bottom sheet covering the mattress and sits Indian-style, holds the flashlight in one hand and with the other, opens the comic...

·*Two young lovers come together over a book... outside the library, an asteroid is seen hitting the city.*

·*During the balmy summer night, a mob of city worker's and citizen have gathered around a crater that pulsates light.*

·*The young lovers walk hand-in-hand through the library's park, unaware in their limerence of the chaos surrounding them.*

·*With industrial lights illuminating the crater, onlookers are brought to by the roar of what is to come: a giant rhino beetle stands upright at nearly forty feet tall.*

·*Eating a late dinner at an outdoor-seated restaurant, the young lovers order their meals while the server and fellow customers watch as police cars, fire trucks, and ambulances speed down the street with sirens blaring.*

·*Following dinner, they find themselves seated in an empty second-run movie theater, paying attention not to the screen, but to one another... exploring with hands and mouths.*

·*The young woman drags the young man toward the door, pupils dilated and an assertive mannerism, as a large stag beetle bursts through the movie screen behind them.*

·*Police open fire on the giant rhino beetle as it snatches and chews an onlooker, while behind the monster, a second giant rhino beetle stands upright.*

·*Holding their ground as the citizens scatter, the police use the doors and rears of vehicles for cover, to shoot an array of pistols, carbines, and shotguns at the beetles to no avail.*

·*With bodies in their grasps, the rhino beetles escape the crater as the smaller, faster dog-sized stag beetles rush*

out and chase after any and all humans with a ravenous
aggression.

·The stag beetles rip and tear flesh and bone from
fleeing civilians and law enforcement in an orgy of gore and
destruction with the rhino beetles knocking over streetlights
and crushing cars with their massive size.

·In the young man's apartment, the young lovers make
love on the couch, tinted grey as the screen of the muted
television and sounds of Electric Wizard from the iPod dock
douse them with sounds of stoner-metal and images from
Them!

The young boy reading the comic book is put off,
perplexed by the sexual manner of the last page's last panel.
He's seen such things but never understood them and finds
it difficult to continue, though his attention is caught on the
woman's breasts he feels an uneasiness.

He continues...

·Stag beetles scramble down streets, bringing down
humans to devour.

·With Electric Wizard's "Barbarian" track filling the
living room, the young couple pleasuring one another are far
from noticing the stag beetle creep in from the open
window... grain of greyness from Them! temporarily
transforming the monster into a 1950's radioactive mutant.

·An officer screams as he is disemboweled by a stag
beetle atop the hood of his police cruiser.

·The original giant rhino beetle stands victorious upon a crushed car, a roar rumbling from within and blood from its victims smearing its horns and exoskeleton.

·In the early light of the morning, the young lovers traverse the destruction in the streets, driving past moaning victims and survivors pleading for help without notice.

·On the highway, their car passes a convoy of National Guardsmen heading toward the city: Humvees, Strykers, jeeps, tanks and troop support vehicles.

·In the downtown streets, soldiers walk beside vehicles, spraying bullets at charging stag beetles and roasting those whose exoskeletons can't be pierced, as others drag hurt civilians from wreckage.

·Closer to the impact zone, a Humvee turret·mounted machine·gunner spreads .50 caliber rounds into a line of attacking stage beetles, depleting their speed and size in numbers.

·In the Adirondack Mountains of New York, the young lovers' car is parked beside a modern·rustic cabin on a dirt drive surrounded by tall trees and shrubbery.

·A candle is lit on the table, throwing shadows that dance up the walls behind the young lovers who sip wine and dine on maple pecan glazed salmon.

·At the crater, the Guardsmen have created an all·out· assault on the monsters. Soldiers on foot fire from their M4s at stag beetles, while tanks and turret·mounted vehicles fire on the giant rhino beetles.

·As night falls, so do the National Guardsmen by the speed, strength, aggression, and sheer size in number of the beetles.

·*The war wages on throughout the night, muzzles flash and explosions echo along walls of the downtown buildings that remain.*

·*Fighting, fighting, fighting, the monsters dominate and shred apart the numbers of humans during the night.*

·*With morning light rising, soldiers prepare gasmasks while one seeking refuge inside the back of a troop transport vehicle, radios in details.*

·*Badger seven requesting immediate air support! Repeat, badger seven requesting release of the IB! Release the insecticide bomb! Release the IB, release the IB!*

·*From the radio: Aircraft twenty seconds out, repeat, two zero seconds!*

·*A-10 Thunderbolt II Warthogs fly over the city.*

·*The crater explodes and from inside a fog begins to build and spread.*

·*The fog fills the streets and the first giant rhino beetle is engulfed, crashes against a building and falls to the ground, dead.*

·*The second giant rhino beetle soon follows as it falls, crushing cars beneath its massive body.*

·*Guardsmen in gasmasks take aim and drill rounds from their M4s into the twitching, disabled stag beetles.*

·*Piles of stag beetles are set aflame by soldiers with flamethrowers, and others search among the dead monsters to end any signs of life.*

·*Citizens with bandanas, painters and surgical masks rush to the streets.*

·Making their way through the rubble of the city, zigging and zagging past dead bodies of humans and monsters alike, the young lovers drive home.

·They pass soldiers who, with legs on a giant rhino beetle's horn, pose for pictures with their M4s held in the air.

·The young lovers come to stop and park in the lot of the young man's apartment, a mostly unharmed building.

·Children in the lot smash the exoskeleton of a dead stag beetle with baseball bats.

·Entering his apartment, there is a scuttling from the shadow behind the couch and unseen by the young lovers, the lone stag beetle exits the open window and crawls up the side of the building to perch on the ledge and look down on its dead and the chaos they brought to Earth.

...and he closes the comic to see an advertisement for the second in the series of four on the back cover. He reads the month and repeats it in his head to mentally memorize the date. To write it would chance discovery by his mother who frowned upon the illiteracy of comic books.

He peels back the strip of Scotch tape that has affixed itself, opens the mylar bag and carefully slips the comic book inside and seals the flap with the strip of tape.

With the beam of the flashlight dying, growing dimmer by the moment, he takes one final good look at the advertisement for issue number two and crawls out from under the sheet and blanket.

The ten-year-old boy hides the comic book under the copy of Mark Twain's *The Adventures of Huckleberry Finn* and shuts off the flashlight, placing it, too, inside the bedside stand and closes the drawer.

In the darkness, within the haze between wakefulness and sleep he relives the panels.

They come alive...

The Young Man and the Young Woman stare into one another's eyes as they embrace; the Rhino Beetle releases its *ROOAAHHAARRR* as it crests the tip of the crater; the Young Woman's breasts; the soldiers scream as their machineguns fire, and the boy's eyes close and he falls asleep with a smile on his face.

IMAGINARY WORLDS

Inside us, there is an imaginary world. A small town with a park full of flowers, ponds and willow trees and a home with two people to hold memories and enact fantasies. Those memories that haunt, those too joyful to keep in this world as they pertain to times of true happiness that bring along with them an equalization: the reality that they're gone... the good times and, that they've been replaced by distance and sobering silence. Fantasies enacted by two imaginary beings, perhaps a young man and a young woman who bear a striking resemblance to the body of the mind and the body of the mind's devotion. Here in this world they live in laughter and love, keeping one another sane and warm, giving fulfillment to each other's lives and knowing that no matter how their individual days may have been, that each night they will crawl into bed and fall asleep with the one. The one person, that one person with whom they share an unspoken bond, a profound and almost numinous understanding of all things and makes them feel complete. A kindred spirit... their kindred spirit.

Inside all of us there is an imaginary world. We go there from time to time to stay safe. To find ourselves and to seek and live out that which we cannot have in this world of ours.

A Summertime Nightmare

When summertime falls asleep, I wonder... does it suffer a reoccurring nightmare of flowers dying, their petals twirling with the chill autumn breeze... twirling, falling to the crisp brown grass?

AUGGIE

Smell is scared? Smell is sad?

They hold mom's hand. Pet her head. Speak to her.

Mom cries.

Other ones cry. Not male. Male does not cry.

Male looks at me. Speaks my name. Speaks to little female. Little one comes. Speaks my name. "Good boy. Good ol' Auggie. I love you. Yes, I do. I love you." Scratches my head. Pets me. Pats my belly. Little one pets me when here.

Big female comes. Pets little one. Hugs little one. Speaks to little one. Female pets me. Little one hugs me. Kisses my nose. "Good Auggie. Love you, boy."

They go away.

Me. Mom. Male.

They speak. I watch. Listen. Smell has changed. Not sad.

Angry.

Smell is bad.

Smell is bad. They speak loud. Mom cries. I jump on bed. Lie down next to mom.

Male watches me. I am bad. Am on bed. Male watches me. Smell is bad.

Mom pets my head. I kiss her. Male speaks my name. Mom speaks.

I can lie here.

I lay my head on mom. My head moves up. Moves down. Mom pets my ear.

Mom smells happy.

I want to sleep.

Mom speaks to male. Male speaks to mom. Mom cries. My head moves up. Male pets me. My head moves down. Male is sad. Happy.

Male is sad? Happy?

I pick up my head. Look.

Mom is sleeping.

Male speaks. "Good ol' Auggie. Good ol' Auggie." Male cries. Kisses mom. Stands. Cries. Smells sad. Walks away.

Male is sad.

Mom is sleeping. I kiss her. Lie my head on her belly. Wait for her to wake up. Fall asleep.

Noise wakes me. New male comes.

I jump.

New male smells scared. He stays.

I guard mom.

Scared.

Proud.

I speak. I growl at new male. He stays.

Male speaks loud. Smells sad. Angry.

I speak. Male speaks loud. Pulls me off bed. Holds my collar. Speaks to new male.

Male walks me. New male smells scared. Touches mom. I growl. Speak. Male puts me outside.

Little one speaks my name. "Auggie. Come here Auggie!"

I run to little one. Holds me. Walks me to my tree. I sit. Little one speaks to me. Pets my belly. Little one smells sad. Happy. Angry.

Bigger female walks inside. I sit. Watch house. Wait for mom. Little one holds me. Pets me.

I wait for mom. Lie down.

Little one lies on me. Pets my head.

My belly is sick. I eat grass.

I want to sleep. Wait for mom.

Want to sleep.

Wait for mom.

I eat grass.

Belly is sick.

SYMPATHY OR SELFISHNESS?
(For Chino. Keep chasing those bunnies, buddy.)

He slumps his worn head on my lap, my legs crossed underneath me on the wooden floor. I stroke his head and I know he understands something is different this time. From my caress, he can sense my sorrow and from his big chapped nose he can smell the concern upon my being. His eyes close for a moment and he yawns: a big bold mug with yellow teeth and black gums, a long dry tongue hoarse from thirst. And in this brief display of exhaustion I can't help but hope that tonight will be the night he passes.

ABOUT THE AUTHOR

Dustin LaValley was unable to attend the black-tie gala to receive the SUNY Parnassus Award for Creative Writing, as he had a fight in New Hampshire the same night, where he brought home gold. He's had several books published, and as a screenwriter several scripts produced. His psychological thriller novella The Deceived, has been optioned for film. He lives in the Adirondacks of New York, where he's a practicing Sensei of Seito Shito Ryu karate and Okinawan jujutsu.

Coming Soon

Exorcist Falls by Jonathan Janz

People of the Sun by Jason Parent

There is Darkness in Every Room by Brian Fatah Steele

Find these and other horrific books at
www.sinistergrinpress.com